Yaakov the Pirate Hunter

NATHANIEL WYCKOFF

Text copyright © 2010, 2015, 2017 by Nathaniel Wyckoff

Cover art by Jeanine Henning
www.jeaninehenning.com

ISBN-10: 1456452495
ISBN-13: 978-1456452490

Third edition, 2017

DEDICATION

This book is dedicated to my beloved children, who inspire me daily, and to my ever-faithful wife, Janna, my truest friend.

I also dedicate this book to my wonderful, loving parents, who grounded me with a true sense of identity and a love of Judaism, and who sparked within me the love of storytelling that made this entire effort possible.

CONTENTS

ACKNOWLEDGMENTS

This work would not have been possible without the instruction and guidance of the Institute of Children's Literature. What started as a relatively simple story about the return of a stolen object, written as a course assignment, blossomed into my first completed children's novel.

My parents laid the very foundation for a story such as this one to exist. From a very young age, I heard fascinating stories from both of them, rich tales drawn from our vast Jewish heritage and creative, invented stories that entertained and educated my two dear brothers and me. My mother has always had a talent for making Judaism come alive, and scarcely a bedtime passed without a fantastic tale from my father. I am forever indebted to them for sparking my lifelong interest in my Jewish identity and tradition, and in storytelling in general.

My children provided this story's motivation. Our innumerable drives to school in the morning were filled with wondrous tales, sparked by their ideas and told by their father as we trekked down La Brea Avenue. Thank you, children, for suggesting stories about robots!

Two friends, Larry Shiver and Eric Golub, provided valuable encouragement regarding my venture into writing and publishing. I am grateful for your continued support and friendship.

I owe a debt of gratitude to a fellow author, Rebecca Klempner, for her advice on producing this edition of *Yaakov the Pirate Hunter*, and on writing in general. She has been a trusted family friend and supporter over the years, and her blog (http://rebeccaklempner.com) and articles have been valued sources of insight.

Last, but far from least, I offer my heartfelt thanks to my wife, Janna, for her unwavering devotion. She has stood by me throughout the entire development of this story and the writing of this book. Her insights, proofreading, comments, questions, and suggestions were invaluable, as I produced both the first and second editions. Thank you for believing in me.

Reviews of *Yaakov the Pirate Hunter*

"★★★★★ Nathaniel is a creative writer with a vivid imagination. Not only does he create vivid worlds you're excited to explore, but he does it in a way that children can grasp and understand the magnitude of the novel concepts and story lines he weaves."

"★★★★★ I read Yaakov the Pirate Hunter with my kids and it was a remarkable experience. Each night my kids waited for me at bedtime to find out what new and exciting storylines would be revealed on that night."

"★★★★★We read it aloud with my six year old son, and he loved it! We couldn't put the book down. Engaging plot, fun adventure. We loved how the story is set in the future, with all the technological advances. (And I'm looking forward to the time when I can buy one of those robots!) My son really liked the pirates' names."

"★★★★★□(Yaakov) the Pirate Hunter is a really fun and exciting futuristic book with a unique twist: the story features (Yaakov) Peretz (11) and his whole family, who are (observant) Jews and their team of highly trained (I mean programmed) robots! The story is very well-written. Kids will enjoy reading this book themselves of having it read to them- especially those who love hi-tech adventure!"

Visit the author website:
http://www.peretzadventures.com

1 THE MAP IN OUR ROBOT

The shiny red disc sailed through the air, reflecting a glint of southern California sunlight as it coasted toward Yosef Peretz's raised hands. "Got it!" he yelled toward his older brother, Yaakov, who stood at the other end of the Peretz family's grassy backyard. "Try not to throw it so high next time. It could have gone on the roof!"

"Sorry," muttered Yaakov, with a shrug. Yaakov didn't worry much about losing a Frisbee on the roof. It would have been easy enough to get. If it landed close enough to the edge, he could simply climb up a nearby lemon tree, reach over, and knock it down or grab it. He had retrieved many a stray baseball and soccer ball that way. Even losing a toy on the very top of the roof was no big deal these days, thanks to the latest member of the Peretz family's workforce of robots.

Yaakov loved to explore the world around him, both by experiencing new things and by reading. His parents encouraged his sense of adventure, through a combination of family trips and books on practically every subject. By age eleven, Yaakov had already traveled with his family to countless museums, science centers, amusement parks, skating rinks, hiking trails, observatories, and zoos throughout the Southland.

Once in a while, Yaakov was happy to enjoy a lazy summer day like this one, playing or relaxing in the yard. The yard was a peaceful retreat, a place where time itself seemed to slow down. At one end, a towering plum tree cast its long shadows over the deep green lawn. In the summertime, Yaakov could pick up a juicy fallen plum from the grass and munch on it while reading a book or just thinking. Directly across from this tree, about forty feet away, grew a much shorter lemon tree. It stood very near to a wall of the house, and was easy to climb. All three Peretz children had scaled it many times.

Yaakov almost tripped over his little sister's bike while sprinting to catch Yosef's next toss of the Frisbee. Why couldn't Rachel have just put it away when she was done with it? he wondered briefly. The Frisbee had started on a straight enough course, but a sudden breeze had picked it up and carried it toward the wooden fence separating their property from the neighbors' yard. Yaakov grabbed the Frisbee out of the air just in time.

"Get ready, Yosef!" called Yaakov. He rolled the tiny bike aside and prepared to throw the Frisbee again. This time, he tried to aim a little lower. If he snapped his wrist just so, he calculated, then he could get the disc to arrive at a point just above his younger and shorter brother's nose. . .

"Not on the roof again!" cried Yosef as the Frisbee

came to rest. "Why do you keep throwing things up there? You know how long it takes to keep going up there and getting them! That's our only Frisbee now, since you threw the little white one into the ocean last week and Rachel took the purple one to the park and lost it."

"I was just trying to master that new throw that my friend Avi taught me a few days ago," Yaakov explained, calmly. He demonstrated a strange-looking gesture with his wrist. "You see? If you let go of the Frisbee as soon as you flick your wrist that way, it. . ."

"Goes flying out of control," interrupted Yosef, shooting Yaakov one of his scowls that seemed more frequent in recent weeks. "Well, now we're stuck without any." He pointed to a high spot on the roof, above the lemon tree. "There it is, too high for anyone to reach it. You can barely even see it from here."

Although he didn't care to admit it, Yaakov dreaded the thought of actually climbing onto the roof himself. Worse still was the prospect of spending the rest of the day avoiding his irritated nine-year-old brother's insults and temper tantrums. He and Yosef stared at each other for a silent moment. A distant drone aircraft soon broke the quiet as it buzzed overhead, probably delivering groceries to an elderly lady in Orange County. Think positive, Yaakov, he told himself. He reminded himself of his father's oft-repeated motto: "There's always a solution."

Yaakov suddenly broke out into a confident smile and began speaking excitedly. "Don't worry, Yosef. I know just the thing to get that Frisbee back down: AutoRiser!" AutoRiser was the newest of the family's robots, a climbing machine purchased just two weeks earlier.

Yaakov turned around and ran to the garage. Its wide front door creaked a bit as Yaakov pulled it upward to open it. He stepped into the shadowy, dusty room and approached the silent row of six roughly humanoid-looking metallic robots standing along its back wall. Each robot was at least two inches taller than he, and possessed its own rare set of abilities. With a smooth and practiced motion, Yaakov approached the second robot from the right, reached around its body and flicked its power switch. AutoRiser immediately came to life, making a series of loud beeps.

"Hello, I'm AutoRiser," came the unnaturally soothing voice from the robot's speakers. The robot extended its right hand and turned its head to face Yaakov. "A pleasant mid-morning to you, sir."

"AutoRiser, follow me," replied Yaakov. "I've got a job for you."

He began walking toward the garage's open doorway. AutoRiser predictably followed him, taking slow and deliberate steps. I'm like a king leading his most trusted general into battle, thought Yaakov, marching back toward the house.

Home robots were all the rage these days, a new and exciting technology that granted instant bragging rights to any child on the playground whose family was lucky enough to own one. When it came many other things that the Peretz children wanted, they were long used to hearing their parents' refrains: "You don't need that," "I don't want to spend money on that right now," and "You have something just like it already." But robots were different. Almost every day, Yaakov's father reminded him and his siblings how fortunate they were to receive such generous deals from their local robot dealer, Dilip Sitoop; most families didn't seem to own more than one or two robots, and the Peretzes now had six.

Yaakov had been fascinated by robot technology for most of his young life. Among his earliest memories was a family trip to the Columbia Memorial Space Center in Downey. At that hands-on, interactive museum, a five-year-old Yaakov had become intrigued by the idea of controlling life-like machines that obeyed his every command. He had played with metallic robot arms, using them to lift green balls, move them around a glass chamber, and then drop them. Yaakov had practiced those moves repeatedly, persisting even long after his three-year-old brother had given up. He had also experimented with the Space Center's planetary rover exhibit. There, children programmed small vehicles to perform sequences of steps, including driving to specific locations, picking up rocks, and depositing them elsewhere. And in a spacecraft simulator, his parents had helped him pretend to land an automated probe on an asteroid to collect mineral samples.

As he matured, Yaakov's love of all things robotic grew with him, and his parents were all too happy to help him learn more. He read books describing robots built to look exactly like their inventors, with strangely human-like voices. Some such devices were able to play sports or to hold fairly realistic conversations. His parents allowed him repeatedly to watch old NASA videos of the planetary rovers that explored the surface of Mars (and were probably still working, as far as Yaakov knew). Even more exciting was the opportunity to build his own automated machines. Year after year, Yaakov begged his parents to buy him toy robots and robot construction kits as birthday and Hanukkah gifts. Building robots eventually became Yaakov's favorite activity. Self-guided dinosaurs and remote-controlled tarantulas began to clutter his bedroom, and his father sometimes joked about charging them rent. Those fairly simple playthings later gave way to more sophisticated devices, machines that obeyed commands received from his mother's laptop. With practice, Yaakov learned how to use them to perform simple chores for him. Why put away his own shoes, he reasoned, when a machine could be taught to do it? Daily, Yaakov dreamed up new ways to make life easier using artificial "personal assistants," and today was no different.

"Oh, come on," Yosef remarked, rolling his eyes as Yaakov emerged from the garage with AutoRiser not far behind. "You really expect that piece of junk to be able to go up there and grab it?" Yosef's scornful response was as disappointing as it was expected. For some reason, he didn't yet seem to appreciate the value of keeping these helpful gadgets around.

Yaakov shrugged again. "Why not? That's what it's supposed to do. Don't worry. Imma and Abba won't mind. Last night I asked them if I could do stuff with the robots today, and they said yes." The Peretz children referred to their mother by the Hebrew word "Imma," and called their father "Abba," as commonly done in many traditional Jewish families.

He faced the five-and-one-half-foot tall climbing machine. "Ready, AutoRiser? Go climb up this wall, then get on the roof and find the red Frisbee. Pick it up and climb back down with it. Then give it to Yosef."

Yosef made an annoyed face and sat down on a large, smooth boulder. His brother stood next to him, feeling a bit anxious. The two of them stared as their robot scaled the wall of their house. Yaakov could tell that his brother was getting impatient.

"This is boring, Yaakov," he complained. "Why did you send AutoRiser up there anyway? That thing's too slow! Why don't you just grab a ladder and climb up there to get it yourself? You're the one who threw it there!"

"Just be patient," answered Yaakov. "Look," he added, pointing upward at the roof. "AutoRiser's almost got it. Anyway, what's the rush? We're on vacation." He quickly glanced downward and saw the words "Sun 29-Jun-2025 9:34 AM" glowing back at him from his digital watch. These summer mornings felt like they could drag on forever. It was a rare, relaxing morning for the Peretz children, whose days were usually packed with scheduled activities. Today, there was no school, no summer camp and no pressure. What difference did it make how slowly the robot moved?

"Yeah, and I don't want to waste a whole day of our vacation sitting around and waiting for some silly robot!" answered Yosef. "I have an idea."

He stood up, looked around for a few seconds, and then ran over to a patch of overgrown grass. Quickly, he rummaged through the grass and picked up a hidden baseball. Then, he brought the ball back to the boulder and climbed on top of it. Standing on the boulder, Yosef took aim at the plastic disc on the sloped roof and hurled the ball. Just then, the reliable climbing android grasped the Frisbee. As it did so, the baseball smacked AutoRiser's shiny head with an earsplitting "clank."

Yaakov heard a faint "thud" as their soft lawn broke AutoRiser's fall. "That silly robot of ours was about to bring us back our Frisbee!" a shocked Yaakov cried. "Why couldn't you just let him?"

"It," snapped Yosef. "Because I was tired of waiting for that slow-poke machine. That's why. Come on, forget about that stupid thing and let's keep playing."

AutoRiser lay on its side, seeming a bit dazed. "Here is your new turkey sandwich, Mr. Paper Clip," announced the robot, as Yaakov tried to take the Frisbee from its left hand. An orange butterfly landed on AutoRiser's metal bump of a "nose." "Good evening," AutoRiser slowly and politely addressed the insect. "Shall...we...take...a...stroll...now? There's a new red wagon wait-ing for you." The robot began to pull itself on one knee, but collapsed back onto the ground. "Another satisfied customer!" announced AutoRiser, waving at the butterfly as it flew away.

Yaakov groaned and buried his face in his hands.

Yaakov's seven-year-old sister, Rachel, came running outside with their father, Yehuda Peretz. "What happened, boys?" asked Yehuda. "I thought I saw a falling robot!"

Yehuda was a fun father. He owned and ran Enigmatic, a store specializing in quirky puzzle games, educational toys, books of brain teasers, and similar items. Yaakov and his siblings often hung around at the store after school, messing around with Rubik's Revenge toys or trying to beat each other at Electronic Jenga.

"And what was that loud noise?" yelled Rachel. "Hey, what happened to our AutoRiser? Why is it laying on the grass? Robots don't get tired."

Yaakov gulped.

"We had a little trouble with the robot," explained Yosef, speaking quickly, "but it's not acting too funny. Not really. Maybe its head got a little jumbled. You see, Abba," he said to his father, "I sort of hit it with a baseball, and it fell off the roof. But, like I said, it's nothing we can't fix right away with a screwdriver or something."

"I heard that noise," interrupted Yehuda, his normally cheerful face now looking rather stern. "I didn't see what happened, but now there are two boys out here standing in front of a broken robot...an *expensive* broken robot."

"Abba, I think I can fix AutoRiser," said Yaakov. "After all, I did build Digital Drudge all by myself. AutoRiser can't be that much more complicated." Digital Drudge was Yaakov's proudest invention. Yaakov liked it to accompany him whenever he needed to get things done. Yosef generally referred to it as "your useless pet."

Yehuda peered directly at Yaakov. "All right. Fix it." He then turned to Yosef. "*Both* of you. *Now.*"

"I want to help!" yelled Rachel excitedly. "I'll get my toolbox!" She turned around and dashed into the house.

"Good idea, Rachel," Yehuda yelled toward her from behind. "And I'll get mine." Turning toward his sons, he added, "Stay right here, boys."

With Rachel's "help," and under their father's watchful eye, Yaakov and Yosef soon managed to open

AutoRiser's head. Yaakov stared at the complicated mess of electronic circuitry that directed all of the robot's activities. Almost immediately, he noticed that several circuit boards were out of place. Clearly, they had been jarred by the collision with Yosef's baseball.

"Abba, look at that," said Yaakov cautiously, pointing to the shaken electronics.

"Those circuit boards must have knocked out of place when AutoRiser landed on the ground, or when the ball hit it," answered Yehuda. "You're the robot builder, Yaakov. Why don't you try moving them back into place?"

Careful not to do any further damage, Yaakov grasped one circuit board and began to nudge it slowly, trying to ease it back into its former position. As he finally clicked it into place, he noticed a bright light shining from the 2-D picture projector in the robot's right electronic eye. A strange image suddenly appeared on the smooth, white wall in front of the Peretzes.

"Well, what have we here?" asked Yehuda in a surprised voice, pointing at the image. On the wall there appeared to be a map displaying a section of the Mojave Desert. The map was rotated sideways. In one corner of the map, a large, sloppy "X" had been drawn in red ink. "We've found some sort of a map. It looks like it might even be a treasure map. In old stories, 'X' often marked the spot on a map showing where pirates had buried their treasures. Some of those stories might even be true."

Yaakov stared at the map. "I don't get it. Why would there be a pirates' treasure map in our robot's head?" he asked.

"Good question," answered Yehuda. "Maybe we

should ask Mr. Sitoop. I'll call him right away."

Yehuda Peretz hurried inside, Yaakov following. He watched as his father picked up his smartphone from the living room table and called Dilip Sitoop. "Hello, Dilip," Yehuda said. "It's Yehuda Peretz. Is everything all right? You sound a little tense. . .Okay. Anyway, I've got something interesting to tell you. You'll never believe what we discovered this morning!" Yehuda turned to Yaakov. "Please wait outside for a few minutes, Yaakov, while I talk to Mr. Sitoop."

Yosef and Rachel tossed around a football while Yaakov sat and stared glumly at the damaged AutoRiser. After several minutes, Yehuda came outside again. The children gathered around him on lawn chairs while their father related a bizarre and amazing story.

"A few weeks ago, Mr. Sitoop witnessed a robbery at the home of a billionaire in Santa Barbara. He was at that man's house to install a robotic chef. A gang of pirates broke into the kitchen, stole a case of expensive jewelry and then escaped from the police by fleeing to the desert. Somehow, they managed to outrun the cops and to bury the stolen treasure. They drew this map to help them remember where to find it when they come back for it later. Mr. Sitoop secretly chased the pirates, following them in his little car as they drove off in an old van. He saw one of the pirates hold up that treasure map and stare at it. That was Mr. Sitoop's big chance. He quickly picked up a little camera and took a picture of their map. Later, he uploaded the photo into one of the robots in his store. But he was so nervous about the whole thing that he forgot which one. Guess which robot it turned out to be?"

"AutoRiser!" Rachel cried.

"That's right, Rachel," replied Yehuda. "Mr. Sitoop's plan was to give back the treasure chest himself, but since we found the pirates' map, he asked us to go and get it for him."

The whole story sounded rather odd to Yaakov. "Why would a gang of pirates break into a house? Don't they usually attack ships?"

"And, why would they make a map?" Yosef contributed. "That was a pretty dumb idea."

"More great questions, boys," answered Yehuda. "First, of all, it sounded like those pirates somehow knew just where to find that chest. They were in and out of the house very quickly. The map was a nice touch. It was actually a clever way to hide their stolen goods. Think about it. Not many people know how to read maps these days, especially not road maps."

"What's a road map?" asked Rachel, with a squint.

"I'll show you one." Yehuda got up from his chair and walked into the garage. He emerged a few moments later, holding a paper, folded into a thick stack. As he walked back to his lawn chair, the children stood up and gathered around him. He began to unfold the paper, and held it in front of the children, who gave him their attention. "This map shows the streets around our house."

"They don't look like streets," said Rachel.

"Well, let me explain it," continued Abba. "Suppose you wanted to get from our house to that new Middle Eastern place that just opened up in Sherman Oaks. What do they call it?"

"Babylon Grill," answered Yosef.

"Okay." Yehuda pointed to a white line on the map,

and moved his finger along the paper as he spoke. "So, here's our street. Now, Babylon Grill is on Ventura Boulevard, all the way over there. The map shows us that, to get there, we'd have to drive over to Highland Avenue, get on the 101, get off at Van Nuys, and then make a right on Ventura."

Rachel gave him a quizzical look. "Abba, why can't we just the tell the car where to take us? It always knows where to go."

"That's true, Rachel," explained Yehuda, in a patient voice. He always seemed to slow down when explaining something, and Yaakov never remembered his father getting annoyed by a childish question. "Our car is pretty new. But, older cars didn't always have built-in directions. People had to look up their directions on maps and figure out how to drive to the places where they wanted to go. It used to be that everybody kept paper maps in their cars, like this one. Then, they started putting maps into cell phones and building direction finders into cars. Those devices would tell people where to turn and where to stop. Today, we can get into a newer car like ours and just tell it an address."

"Well, what if you just wanted to go to some random spot with no address, and you didn't exactly know how to get there?" asked Yosef.

Yehuda tapped the road map. "Then, you would need one of these."

Yaakov leapt from his chair and began to talk excitedly. "So, the pirates drew a map to some place in the desert, and weren't too careful about hiding it, because they figured that nobody else would be able to read their map anyway. I think we should go find that stolen treasure and return it!" The idea of getting involved with pirates was a scary one, but Yaakov knew that it was an important *mitzvah*, a commandment from the Torah, to return a lost or stolen object to its rightful owner.

"I think you're right," replied Yehuda. "We've got the map, so we're the right people to find and return the treasure. Mr. Sitoop can't do it. He's pretty shaken up right now, because he suspects that one of the pirates saw him, and he's afraid they might be spying on him. He doesn't even want to leave his house, even though he has to sometimes. What do you say, kids? How does a long drive to the desert sound today?"

"Fun!" exclaimed Rachel. "Can I bring my sand toys?"

"Sure," answered Yehuda with a smile. "And what do you say, Yosef?"

Yosef eyed his father with a look of annoyance. "I get the front seat," he replied.

2 THE ADVENTURE BEGINS

Their white, all-electric SUV drove itself northeast down the 15 freeway, moving more deeply into the parched Mojave Desert with each passing moment. The vehicle was loaded with bottles of water, snacks, shovels, and the three robots that occupied its back seat. AutoRiser, now repaired to the best of Yaakov and Yosef's abilities, sat at one end. Next to it sat Explor-aton, the Peretzes' trusty guide, designed for navigating trips both long and short, as well as uncovering hidden locations. Explor-aton was essential on a trip like today's. The vehicle's built-in GPS device would not have been able to find this buried treasure, since the pirates' map included neither street intersections nor addresses. AutoShoveler, a robotic digging machine, was perched at Explor-aton's right. In the middle row sat a sleeping Rachel and a wide-awake Yaakov, who stared out the right passenger side window at the rocky scene around him, lost in thought. What a strange and exciting Sunday today was turning out to be. Treasure hunts didn't happen every day. Yaakov couldn't wait to tell his friends that he had traveled to the desert with a real treasure map to find a fortune stolen and buried by actual pirates!

Pirate stories always seem to occur overseas, in faraway lands and in ancient times. Yaakov had read and heard stories of characters like Long John Silver and Bluebeard, who sailed the high seas on old-style wooden ships, drank rum by the bottle and fired cannonballs at their enemies. Some of them carried parrots on their shoulders, and all of them loved to hunt for, and to steal, other people's property. Yaakov's parents had told him stories of more recent pirates who rowed from the shores of Somalia on tiny rowboats and attacked sailing ships from nearly every country in the world, kidnapping passengers and holding them for high ransoms. Even those pirates were now ancient history, like floppy disks, DVD players and landline telephones. The closest thing that Yaakov had ever seen to a real pirate was a mechanical puppet on the "Pirates of the Caribbean" ride at Disneyland. The idea of a real, live gang of pirates robbing a wealthy man in California seemed too wild to believe. Maybe Mr. Sitoop had made up the whole story, he mused. Maybe those pirates made a fake map just to trick Mr. Sitoop, but really buried their stolen treasure in a completely different place. . .

"When are we gonna get there already?" a bored-looking Yosef asked from the front passenger's seat as the little green clock on the dashboard struck 12:00.

"Explor-aton can tell us how close we are," answered Yehuda Peretz.

"I'll ask him – I mean, I'll ask it," offered Yaakov.

"Do it quietly," said Yehuda in a hushed voice. "You're sister's sleeping."

"No problem," whispered Yaakov. From his pocket, he pulled out his BotConv, a robot-signaling device, and attached it to his left ear. Then, he turned to face Explor-aton and continued whispering. "Explor-aton, how do we get from here to the 'X' on the map? Show me the directions."

The robot's colorful screen instantly lit up, displaying a close-up view of a small portion of AutoRiser's map. Overlaid on the pirates' crude drawing, the freeway appeared as a wide strip of gray stretching from the bottom left corner to the top right corner of Explor-aton's screen. A small, white moving blip on the gray strip showed the location of the family car, and a blue dotted arrow pointed away from the road, toward the red "X" on the map.

Yaakov heard a soft voice in his left ear. "Turn right in six minutes and thirteen seconds."

"Soon we have to turn right, Abba," whispered Yaakov.

"Okay, Yaakov," answered Yehuda, also whispering. "Just tell me when. I'll have to put the car in manual mode."

A short while later, Yehuda pulled the vehicle to a stop. The children clambered out, and stood in the sand next to their father. AutoRiser then left the SUV, and Explor-aton soon followed it.

"Explor-aton, where was that 'X' on the map?" asked Yaakov, as soon as the robot had set its foot in the sand.

Explor-aton stepped several paces ahead and then stopped. It raised an arm and pointed to a spot where the earth seemed softer and looser than the rest of the hard desert ground. Obviously, somebody had recently done some digging there and loosened the dirt. Yaakov looked around. The desert stretched for miles in every direction. It was a flat, whitish-brown landscape dotted by occasional low shrubs and extending as far as the eye could see. This scene was broken only by the gray highway that cut through it and by the mountains visible in the distance. The air was perfectly still, and the noontime sun beat down without mercy. It was difficult to believe how quiet it was. The city of L.A. never seemed so serene.

His father broke the silence with a command to AutoShoveler. "AutoShoveler, turn on your metal detector. Then start digging at that spot, where Exploraton is pointing. Just keep digging until you pick up a signal. We'll take over then, to make sure the treasure doesn't get damaged."

AutoShoveler dug a hole in the ground, while the children and their father sat nearby, drinking bottled water and watching the robot work. It only took about ten minutes for AutoShoveler's metal detector to begin making noises. The robot climbed out of its four-foot hole, stood next to it, lifted its shovel, and declared, "Welcome to your new hole."

"Thanks, AutoShoveler," answered Yehuda. "Go back into the car and sit down." Then, he turned to the children. "Kids, make sure you're not thirsty, and let's get to work."

"Wait a minute, Abba," said Yosef. "If that robot's such a great digger, then why don't we just let it dig up the jewels for us?"

Yehuda looked at Yosef and pretended to be

disappointed. "Now, that wouldn't be much fun, would it? We came here to hunt for buried treasure, didn't we? Come on, kids. Bring your shovels, and let's. . .*dig in*!" Then, he chuckled to himself, seemingly amused by his own hilarious pun.

"Dig in," repeated Yosef to himself, in a childish, mocking voice. He sat down and absent-mindedly began playing with the sand.

Yaakov and Rachel eagerly joined their father in widening and deepening AutoShoveler's original hole. The three of them shoveled away the dirt as quickly as their arms would allow. Yaakov often had to pause, wiping the sweat off of his forehead and brushing away the dripping sunscreen before it seeped into his eyes. What did I get myself into when I offered to fix AutoRiser? he scolded himself. It's nice to do a mitzvah and to help someone, but it is it worth it to work so hard on a Sunday afternoon, digging in the desert for a treasure that might not even be there?

After about fifteen minutes, Yaakov felt tired, thirsty and discouraged. As he dug, he imagined a tall glass of ice-cold lemonade in front of him, squeezed from the family's homegrown lemons. At that moment, the drink seemed more important than some mysterious box of another family's stolen jewels. He looked up from the ditch and faced his father, ready to ask him if everybody could just go home and rest. Just as he started to open his mouth, he heard a loud "clang."

"Hey, I just hit something hard!" yelled Rachel.

Yaakov and Yosef scrambled over, and began helping Rachel to brush aside the sand. Together, the children managed to uncover a dark brown box. Yaakov felt overcome with excitement as soon as he saw it, and soon forgot about his exhaustion and thirst. The three of them pulled at the box.

"Let me help you, kids," said Yehuda. He joined his children in trying to dislodge the box. With a final, hard yank, the box popped out of its spot. The Peretzes stepped out of their ditch and placed the box onto the ground next to it. It was a wooden chest about the size of a small suitcase, with a metal plate on its lid. Faint letters were engraved into the metal. After squinting at the lettering for a few seconds, Yaakov could identify the name "A. Sapir," along with a faded portion of a street address.

"Good work, children!" announced Yehuda. "Now we're real treasure hunters. We've just discovered a buried treasure!"

"Abba, I think I can read the owner's name and address," said Yaakov, "but I've never heard of that street. And it looks like part of it's missing." He read the address aloud. "It looks like '4267 P-A-S', then some blank space and broken letters, and then 'R-O.' There's no city or state."

"Where do you think it is, Abba?" asked Yosef.

"It's hard to say, Yosef," answered Yehuda. "Mr. Sitoop did tell me that the treasure was stolen from Santa Barbara, but we'd better ask Explor-aton to help us find the way. Kids, please help carry this treasure chest back to the car. There are some snacks waiting for you there."

The children helped their father carry the wooden box back to their SUV. Yehuda spoke a voice command, and the vehicle's side door opened. Together, the four of them held up the box in front of Explor-aton's electronic eyes. Within seconds, the robot's screen displayed a street map of an affluent section of Santa Barbara County.

"Another road map," asked Rachel, "right, Abba?"

"Right," answered her father. "Another road map."

"Can you help us read it?" she asked, excitedly.

"Sure," he answered. "The full address is 4267 Paseo de Oro, in Santa Barbara. Paseo de Oro is that long white line, and the owner's house is the one with the blinking dot on it. Those green patches are lawns, and the blue splotches are swimming pools or ponds. Judging by the sizes of those properties, it looks like a very rich neighborhood."

"Abba," said Yaakov, "today we're already treasure hunters. Can we be explorers, too, and head straight to Santa Barbara to bring back the box? Anyways, we've never been there before."

"Wait a minute," said Yosef, "we don't even know what's in it. What if the pirates took all the jewels and then filled up the box with rocks, just to fool people?"

"Yeah, I want to open it!" shouted Rachel. "Maybe there's a pretty necklace inside it that I can give to Imma."

"Rachel," answered Yehuda in a patient tone, "your mother has whatever she needs, so you don't have to do that. Anyway, it would be stealing. The box doesn't belong to us, and neither do the things inside it." He then looked at Yaakov. "I think we can be explorers today, if you really want to take another trip. We can continue our adventure in Santa Barbara. I'll program the car to zip down the road as fast as we're allowed to go. We'll keep the air conditioning on, and we can also eat that fresh watermelon that we packed this morning."

"Abba," asked Yosef, "why bother? Now that we

have the address, we can just mail the package to the owner, right?"

"Well, Yosef," his father answered, "sending a heavy box full of jewels in the mail is a risky idea. If thieves were able to steal these jewels from somebody's house, which was probably locked with a security system, then sending it through the mail isn't safe at all."

"Do you think another trip will be okay with Imma?" asked Yosef. "We're spending the whole day traveling all over the place."

"Yeah," added Rachel, "and I'm tired of sitting in a car all day. Let's go somewhere fun, like Calico Ghost Town!"

"Calico Ghost Town? Aren't we having fun already?" asked Yehuda, loudly, smiling and stretching his arms before him with his palms facing upward.

It was just like Yaakov's father to prefer the hard way of doing something to the easy way. It was also just like him to call the hard way "the fun way." Still, Yaakov felt grateful for having an exciting and adventurous father, even with all the silly puns that he liked to tell.

Yaakov was determined to save the trip. "Yosef, Rachel, remember what Imma said this morning when we wanted to watch her paint that big picture of the city on the mountain? She said, 'Children, go do something outside for a while. I'm busy.' What are we waiting for, Abba? Let's go!"

3 PIRATES WON'T STOP US!

"4267 Paseo de Oro."

Yaakov repeated the address under his breath several times, as the automatic seatbelt buckled him securely into the vehicle's passenger side front seat. The upcoming journey seemed unreal to him. He was about to deliver a stolen treasure to its mysterious owner living on a "Street of Gold."

He watched as his father programmed the street address into the vehicle's automatic navigation system, along with the words "Santa Barbara, California." Now that the Peretzes had an actual street address, both driving and navigating the SUV were automatic processes. Explor-aton was probably irrelevant for the rest of the trip, Yaakov reasoned, but stayed powered on just in case something happened.

The vehicle's engine started, and the long drive to Santa Barbara began.

"Is that street really made of gold, Abba?" asked Rachel from the middle row. "If it is, can we break off some pieces and take them home?"

"No, dear," answered Yehuda, turning his head for a second and smiling at her. "It's just an interesting street name. It must be in one of the richest neighborhoods in the state to have a name like that. Speaking of names, 'Sapir' should sound familiar to you kids, from the labels on some of our Shabbat wine. It also means 'sapphire' in Hebrew. I wonder if this Sapir family is the same one that owns that big winery."

Each week, the Peretzes happily observed *Shabbat*, the weekly Jewish day of rest. For twenty-five hours, from late Friday afternoon until Saturday night, they left electronic devices and motor vehicles off, let their lights run on timers, prayed, studied the Torah, and enjoyed relaxing family time. They also celebrated the day with festive meals that included small amounts of wine and grape juice for everyone. Over the years, Yaakov had started to find some of his parents' wines quite tasty, though he never drank more than a mouthful on any *Shabbat*.

A steady, cool breeze blew from the air conditioning system, and the children snacked on sweet watermelon and fruit juice, as the Peretzes sped through mile after mile of rocky and arid desert. Later, they rushed past the endless stream of houses and tall buildings that made up the city and county of Los Angeles, eventually reaching the California coast. On seeing several scattered boats in the Pacific Ocean, Yaakov was reminded once again of pirates. Though he usually didn't care much about where he sat in the family vehicle, today he was especially happy to be in the front seat, his mind full of questions that he hoped his father could answer.

"Abba, why did Mr. Sitoop call those robbers 'pirates,' anyway?" he asked, as they entered the outskirts of Ventura County. "There's no such thing as a pirate. They're either just made up stories or characters from two hundred years ago. So, whoever stole those jewels must have just been a bunch of ordinary robbers."

"Well," answered Yehuda, "maybe they were a gang of robbers who dressed up as pirates just to scare their victims and to protect themselves. In the past, other criminal gangs have done the same thing. They wanted to be famous – just famous enough to be feared, but not famous enough to get caught. A lot of them ended up famous, but for the wrong reasons."

"Tell us about some, Abba!" called Yosef from the back seat.

"Well," said Yehuda, "one of the silliest ones was the Bozo Bunch, who used to dress up as circus clowns and then go around robbing people." All three children began laughing at the mention of the gang's name, and Yehuda continued. "They were busted when they ran back into a liquor store that they'd just held up, to get some forgotten beef jerky, and a surprised young lady threw her coffee at them. One of those robbers actually took off his clown wig and started using it to fan his burns. And, of course, the others kept slipping on the spilled coffee and howling in pain. That gave the police plenty of time to arrive and arrest them."

"What other weird thieves were there, Abba?" asked Rachel.

"Let's see now," answered Yehuda. He paused to think for a few moments. "Do you want to hear about the Flame Broiled Crew?"

"Yeah!" the children exclaimed in unison.

"Okay," replied Yehuda. "They were a bizarre group of criminals who used to dress up as chefs and terrorize elderly people with spatulas and egg beaters. Their getaway car was an old restaurant delivery truck. One morning, one of those weirdoes accidentally showed his own ID card when he tried to cash one of his victims' Social Security checks, and that was the end of them. Oh, and nobody my age can forget the Cucamonga Seven! Have you ever heard of them, kids?"

"No," answered Yaakov, followed by Rachel.

"Tell us about them, Abba!" exclaimed Yosef.

"Why not?" replied their father. "The Cucamonga Seven were a gang of thugs from Rancho Cucamonga who used to disguise themselves as cuckoo birds while they drove up and down the state on a really weird crime spree. They thought it was funny that 'cuckoo' sounded like 'Cucamonga.' So, they kept trying to steal antique clocks, especially cuckoo clocks, hoping to sell the clocks for high prices on the Internet. They even used to leave a little wind-up cuckoo bird at the scene of every robbery. Finally, a little girl caught one of them breaking into her room, and she shocked him with her own cuckoo clock. The guy jumped out of the second story window and landed in a tree. Before he could escape, the next door neighbor called the police and told them that some loony was stuck there and needed help getting down."

While Yosef and Rachel chattered about how foolish those thieves were, Yaakov sat quietly for a few moments, taking it all in. Then, he asked, "Well, aren't pirates primitive, Abba? How hard can be to catch them? I mean, a bunch of guys with swords and hooks are no match for modern armies and police, right?"

"That's a good question, Yaakov," answered Yehuda. "You'd be surprised to find out that, these days, it's actually getting harder to catch pirates."

"What do you mean?" asked Yaakov.

"Hundreds of years ago," replied Yehuda, "navy sailors would just capture pirates and lock them up. Those pirates would never be able to attack anyone again. The pirates were usually more primitive than the sailors who fought them. But today, many of them are more advanced than they used to be. Even though some pirates are still stuck in the twentieth century, now and then you can still find gangs of them on ships with some pretty advanced equipment and weapons. It takes a lot to fight them, because some of today's pirates can do a lot to fight back.

"Anyway, it looks we're entering Santa Barbara now. Let's find out where this A. Sapir lives."

Before long, the vehicle parked itself next to a freshly mowed, green lawn lined with tall trees in front of a sprawling estate.

"Here we are, kids," announced Yehuda. "Everyone, help me unload the treasure chest. I think we'll have to carry it together again. We can leave the robots in the car."

"Can we bring AutoRiser?" asked Yaakov, anxiously. "I want to. . ."

"What do we need that thing for?" interjected Yosef. "You think it'll have to climb the wall and throw the treasure in through the window?"

Yaakov ignored his brother. "Abba, I want to tell the owner the whole story about how we found his treasure, so I want to show him AutoRiser, because we found the treasure map in its head."

"Fine," said Yehuda, with a stern look, "but just AutoRiser."

The late afternoon sun cast long shadows as Yaakov and family carefully carried the wooden box across the lawn, toward the Sapir home. AutoRiser trundled after its owners. Yaakov pictured himself in an elegant living room, heroically presenting the stolen object to its prosperous and kind owners. Maybe they'll let us keep some of the jewels inside it, he imagined. Even a few of them could be worth a fortune.

Suddenly, a loud shout interrupted his daydream.

"Avast!" Yaakov turned and found himself face to face with a short, grumpy-looking, disheveled man with a scraggly beard. On his head, he wore a striped rag, and he carried a worn pack on his left shoulder. A black patch covered his left eye. Yaakov took a look around, and then gasped as soon as he noticed the other five strange-looking characters, similarly dressed, standing around them. They were surrounded by pirates!

Immediately, Yehuda turned and faced the bearded ringleader. He loudly clapped his hands together in front of him and announced, with a broad smile, "Perfect! Thank you so much for coming. You're just the guys I've been looking for all weekend. We're putting on a production of 'Peter Pan' down at the NoHo Arts District in the Valley, and we're badly in need of extras, especially with summer vacation and all. My kids are still a little young for it, but the six of you? Just what we need. Pity we had to come all the way to Santa Barbara to find you, but it was worth the trip. I can even put in a good word with the director, and get you a speaking part here and there – you know, a 'walk the plank' or two, or another 'avast,' if you prefer. Can I put you down for next Sunday afternoon?"

All three children were now chuckling quietly at their father's sudden, improvised performance. He seemed to have a real talent for relieving tense situations with silly humor.

The bearded man ignored Yehuda and fixed his menacing gaze on Yaakov. "No one messes with Pete Weasel the Pirate," he said in a gravelly voice. "Pete Weasel – that's me, and you're carrying our treasure."

"You're also messing with me, Eyepatch Izzy!" yelled another pirate.

"And me, Red Louie," grunted another.

With anger in their voices, the other three disheveled members of this gang introduced themselves as Barracuda Harry, Jake the Claw, and Powder-keg Fred. It all seemed like a scare tactic.

Pete Weasel continued speaking. "I guess you didn't notice the tiny tracking device that we attached to the bottom of that treasure chest! You think we're a bunch of fools? That tracker told us where our treasure was the whole time. We just followed you here to get it. That treasure's ours. We robbed it from this here house fair and square! Now put it down and walk away, and nobody gets hurt. You'd better listen, or I'll smash this robot of yours to pieces!"

With that, Pete Weasel shoved his right hand into his pack and pulled out a large mallet. At the same time, he grabbed AutoRiser by its left "shoulder" and pulled it close to his chest. He then lifted the mallet and held it several inches from the robot's head. Yaakov and his siblings watched the scruffy pirate's actions in silent horror. Having traveled so far to return the stolen treasure, Yaakov was not about to let these pirates stop him. Yet, he knew that it would be impossible to reach the mansion's front door without somehow getting this gang of thieves to leave him and his family alone. All he needed was a distraction! He muttered a quiet prayer for help.

Just then, Rachel spoke up. "Those pirates make me mad! Who are they to steal the same treasure twice? Hey, Weasel! Why don't you pick on someone your own smell? Leave us alone!"

"Yeah, get back to your cave and swat away the flies from that stinky rag on your head!" yelled Yosef.

An odd idea instantly sprang into Yaakov's mind. He had once read about tsetse flies, unusual, disease-carrying creatures native to Africa. Tsetse flies are dangerous insects that travel in swarms and carry a germ that causes sleeping sickness. Travelers to the tsetse fly's natural habitat are warned to avoid it at all costs. Since pirates roam the world to commit their crimes, Yaakov reasoned that anyone who has been a pirate for even a short while must know something about tsetse flies. Even if the odd characters surrounding Yaakov were only pretending to be pirates, Yaakov figured that they must have done their homework.

Yaakov quickly tapped on the BotConv device still attached to his ear. "Explor-aton," he quietly instructed the robot in the SUV, "search your global image database and find a picture of a Gambian tsetse fly swarm. Project a 3-D hologram of the swarm at the thick tree branches hanging about two feet above AutoRiser. Lower that hologram slowly until it's in front of AutoRiser's head. Make fly-buzzing noises and use your built-in projection speakers to make them sound like they're always coming from the flies."

Suddenly, a buzzing swarm of large, strange-looking winged insects appeared from nowhere. They swooped down from the nearby trees, hovering right before Pete Weasel's face. The head pirate let out a shout, released AutoRiser, dropped his hammer, and began swatting his hands at the illusory insects.

"Help! Get these flies away!" yelled Pete Weasel. His puzzled companions dashed toward their leader. For the moment, the pirates seemed to have forgotten about AutoRiser and its owners. They gathered around Pete Weasel and started trying to help him shoo the imaginary flies away from his head.

Yaakov felt proud of his own newfound courage.

"Run, kids!" yelled his father. "Let's get this treasure to the front door, quickly!"

Still grasping the treasure, the Peretzes broke into a run and continued carrying the Sapirs' box across the vast green lawn. After a few seconds, Yaakov glanced over his shoulder. His eyes met those of Powder-keg Fred for a brief instant.

"Hey, Pete! They're getting away!" thundered the pirate.

"Huh?" replied Pete, looking in the Peretzes' direction. His facial expression changed from confusion back to anger. "Get them!"

Yaakov then turned to his father, as the pirates drew primitive-looking swords and began their chase, leaving AutoRiser behind. "Abba, I think those pirates forgot about our fake tsetse flies."

Suddenly, the mansion's wide front door opened,

and a slender, gentle-looking man stood in the doorway. He was dressed casually, and appeared to be about Yehuda Peretz's age and size. The man seemed bothered by all of the commotion in front of his house. He reached toward a wall with his right hand, apparently pushing a button. Immediately, his private security guards appeared and raced outside. The Sapir Security force quickly caught and arrested all six pirates.

Yehuda turned to Yaakov, as the children and their father arrived at the doorstep. "Good work, Yaakov. Your quick thinking really paid off."

"Thanks, Abba. By the way, are we really putting on a production of Peter Pan?"

"No," his father answered with a smile, "I was just pretending. When you're facing a nutty opponent, you have to act even crazier."

The man at the front door introduced himself as Aharon Sapir. Right away, the three children excitedly began to relate the events of the past day.

"We dug a huge hole in the ground!" yelled Rachel. "It must have been about ten feet deep and ten feet wide. Our digging robot helped us. It's in the car now."

"Yeah," said Yaakov, "my sister's talking about AutoShoveler, our digging robot. It's still in our car." He then turned around and pointed to AutoRiser. "That robot on your lawn is AutoRiser. We found a map to your treasure in its head. The guy who sold us that robot put it there after he saw the pirates rob your house."

"We found the map after AutoRiser fell off our roof," added Yosef.

Mr. Sapir thanked Yehuda and the children

graciously for his returned box of valuables. "Inside that treasure chest are things worth a lot more than their value in money. They're precious to me not because they're expensive, but because they've been in my family for many years, some of them for generations or even centuries. You can't replace such things with money. You kids – with your father's help, of course – have done a great thing for my family by hunting down our jewels and outsmarting those thieves." He paused for a moment and squinted at the defeated pirates who sat on his lawn, being handcuffed by his private security guards. "You know something? Now that those men are sitting right in front of me, I have to say that I recognize them."

"From where?" asked Yaakov, startled.

Mr. Sapir let out a sigh and answered. "Last month was my birthday, and my family threw a big party for me. It was on one of our yachts in the harbor. There, my grandfather gave me that big box of family jewels. He even got up and gave a little speech about entrusting it to me for future generations. Throughout the party, I kept noticing little boats sailing around in the harbor, with strange-looking people on some of them. I asked my wife if she saw anything unusual, but she said she didn't. Those thieves sitting there on my lawn look just like the weird men who went sailing around the harbor last month. I'll bet they were snooping. They saw a big party and figured there was something to steal. They must have followed us home, and then waited a week or two for the right time to strike. I guess I should have been more suspicious when I saw that gray ship with the weird name painted on it: 'Viper of the Sea.'" He sighed again and shook his head.

"I'd like to show you something else, children, and tell you about something even more valuable than those family jewels. Your father can look, too."

Aharon Sapir pulled a grayish object from his back pocket. It looked like a rolled-up piece of paper. He unrolled the object to its full width, so that it took up both of his hands. Yaakov instantly recognized it, having recently read in a magazine about inventions like this one. It was a flexible electronic tablet. Flexible electronic devices were a new development, and Mr. Sapir apparently was among the first to own them. They were built using a substance called graphene, a material made of carbon sheets only one atom thick. With such thin sheets of carbon, electronics engineers were now learning new and exciting ways to make useful devices even easier to build and to carry. Graphene circuits were far easier to bend and to fold than were other types, which commonly included substances such as silicon dioxide or gallium nitride. Some inventors were even promising that, in the near future, common objects like curtains, clothing and shopping bags would include built-in display screens.

The screen on Mr. Sapir's device now showed a colorful geographic map. On it, a small island was visible in a large body of water, close to two bumps jutting up from a large landmass. "You see the island?" Mr. Sapir asked his visitors. "It's called Djerba. Djerba is located off the coast of a country called Tunisia, in northern Africa. My grandfather tells me that there's another family treasure on that island, even more precious than our family jewels. This item is even very important to the people who live on Djerba. But my grandfather says that it's in danger, and has to be protected. It's hard for him to travel these days, and right now is not a good time for me to leave Santa Barbara. You're a good bunch of treasure hunters. How would you like another family adventure? The whole trip will be on me."

"Let's leave right away!" shouted Yaakov. Another adventure! He could hardly wait to tell his mother.

4 SABBA TELLS A STORY

Yaakov, Yosef, Rachel, and their father sank into plush, purple sofa cushions in the lavish living room nestled at the western edge of the Sapir family's Spanish-style estate. The children stared silently at the room around them with wide eyes. Yaakov had never before seen a home decorated with such luxury. Giant paintings of gorgeous landscapes adorned the walls, along with portraits of the family and old photographs of revered ancestors. Much of the furniture looked like it had come from a museum, old but still elegant and useful. As the sun set further in the sky, rays of white sunlight became visible as they crossed through the many glass prisms in the crystal chandelier hanging from the ceiling. Spectacular patterns of rainbow-colored light seemed to decorate the plates of pastries and the cups of tea and juice on the table in front of Yaakov and his family.

Aharon Sapir and his wife, Tamar, sat on fancy armchairs opposite their new friends. "I'd like you to meet my grandfather, Tzadok Sapir," said Aharon, after the children had rested and snacked for a short while. "We call him Sabba Tzadok," he added, referring to his grandfather by the word's Hebrew translation, "Sabba." Aharon continued, "He's been living with us for a long time, and it's been a real blessing. Besides being a wonderful Sabba, he's like a never-ending fountain of knowledge. There's an ancient Torah scroll on that island that I showed you before, and I want you to hear all about it from Sabba Tzadok. Wait here. I'll be right back."

Yaakov thought about that name, Sabba Tzadok, as Mr. Sapir left the living room. "Tzadok" was related to the Hebrew word "Tzedek," meaning "righteousness." "Grandfather Tzadok" must be very special person if he lived up to his name.

Mr. Sapir returned a few minutes later with an elderly, dignified-looking man. The older man was dressed in a modest, grayish-black suit and simple black hat. He walked in sure-footed steps, only slightly bent, with no need to hold onto a cane or onto his grandson's arm. On his bearded face, he wore a pair of thin glasses and a gentle expression. To Yaakov, the man seemed quite holy. Yehuda Peretz and his children stood to honor him, and to greet him, as he entered the room.

"Come have a seat, Sabba," said Mr. Sapir, leading his grandfather to another soft armchair. "I'd like you to meet my new friends, the Peretzes, from Los Angeles. They've done a great *mitzvah* for us today. They found that box of family treasures that those pirates stole a few weeks ago, and they brought it back to us."

"And let's remember that they outsmarted those

pirates and helped us catch them!" added Tamar.

"That's right," said Aharon, with a nod. He looked at the visitors sitting on his purple couch and began introducing them to his grandfather. "This is Yehuda Peretz," he said, pointing to Yaakov's father, "and you kids will have to remind me of your names."

"I think I know their names," said Tamar. She pointed first to Rachel, then to Yosef, then to Yaakov, and named each child for Sabba Tzadok. "You won't forget their names, will you, Sabba Tzadok?"

"My grandfather has a photographic memory," explained Aharon, before his grandfather could answer the question. "He remembers things better than anyone."

"Such a brave family you are indeed," said Tzadok Sapir. "But tell me, where is your mother?"

"She's at home, working on a painting," explained Yehuda. "I noticed the great artwork on these walls. Leah also happens to be a very talented artist. In a couple of weeks, she wants to enter a number of her own landscapes in an art show. It's kept her very busy lately."

"Really?" asked Tamar. "I'd like to meet her some day."

"If she's anything like the father and the kids," said Aharon rather quickly, "then the El-Ghriba Torah scroll is perfectly safe." Turning to Sabba Tzadok, he continued. "Sabba, I've shown our guests a small map of the area around Djerba, and they know that there's a very old Torah scroll there. Would you please tell them more about its history?"

The elder Mr. Sapir sat back in his chair and let out a brief sigh. "Where should I begin? After the

Babylonians conquered the Land of Israel and destroyed the First Temple, the Jewish people were sent into exile. Most of those who survived the destruction were forced to go to nearby countries like Babylonia. Some managed to keep traveling eastward, and even reached places as far away as China. A small group of *Cohanim*, the men who actually served in the Temple, sailed westward, across the Mediterranean Sea.

"Those original *Cohanim* discovered a tiny island called Djerba, and decided to settle there. One of the first things that they did was to build a synagogue. They managed to bring one of the Temple's doors on their journey from Jerusalem, and included it in the building. They also managed to bring a Torah scroll, which every synagogue needs.

"I don't think those *Cohanim* ever expected to stay on Djerba for as long as they did. Over time, more Jews settled on that island. For over 2,400 years, Djerba has had a Jewish community. Many nations have conquered Djerba since then – the Romans, the Muslims, the Spaniards – all of them coming and going, while the Jewish community there survived. A Greek legend describes an 'Island of the Lotus-Eaters,' where people ate lotus leaves that put them to sleep and made them forget about leaving. That legend is actually about Djerba. Today, the island is part of Tunisia. The Jewish community there has lived in peace with its neighbors for many years.

"In the place where Djerba's original synagogue was built, Jews have been praying for many centuries, though the original building isn't there anymore. There's a newer building there now, and the synagogue is called 'El-Ghriba.'"

At this point, Sabba Tzadok leaned forward and looked at the Peretzes with a very serious gaze. Yaakov sat up straight and paid close attention. "Not many people know this," he continued, "but that original Torah scroll still rests inside the El-Ghriba synagogue. Many empires have come and gone, and that piece of Jewish history has outlived them all."

"That's an amazing story," said Yehuda, "but what does it have to do with us?"

"I'm glad you asked," said Sabba Tzadok. "You know that every *Cohen* is a descendant of the original one, Aharon the *Cohen*."

"I'm named after him," said Aharon. "Sorry to interrupt, Sabba. Please continue."

"I happen to come from the original group of *Cohanim* who settled on Djerba more than 2,400 years ago. In fact, an ancestor of mine wrote down the ancient Torah scroll that still sits in the El-Ghriba synagogue today. It's the oldest Torah in the world. I'm afraid that right now, that ancient Torah scroll, that piece of Jewish history – and family history – is in danger."

"What danger?" asked Yaakov, fascinated by the tale.

"Do you remember that gang of pirates who met you outside today? How many were there?" asked Sabba Tzadok.

"Six," answered Yaakov with pride. He still felt quite heroic about having foiled their plans.

"Six," repeated Sabba Tzadok. "But they were part of a gang of at least seven. In fact, when this house was robbed three weeks ago, a gang of seven pirates broke in, not only six. Follow me to the kitchen and I'll show you what happened. I still remember it quite well."

YAAKOV THE PIRATE HUNTER

He stood up, motioned for the others to follow, and began walking down the hallway that led to the estate's main kitchen.

"Aharon and I were out of the house when the robbery happened," Tamar told the Peretzes as they followed Sabba Tzadok's lead, "so we don't know about it firsthand, but we trust Sabba Tzadok to remember all the details. He really does recall everything he sees and hears, exactly as it happens."

"Abba, what's that?" asked Rachel, entering the kitchen and pointing at a large metal device hanging from the ceiling. "It looks like a toy spider!" Her brothers and father soon gazed upward at a can-shaped machine with long, silvery legs connected to it at many points around its outside.

"A big one!" added Yaakov. "I'll bet we could ride it, too."

"That's the weirdest piece of playground equipment I've ever seen," commented Yosef. "Do you untie from the ceiling and carry it outside every time you want to use it? And why do you keep it in the kitchen?"

"That, my friends," announced Aharon Sapir with a wide smile, "is our new Kitchen Caesar Deluxe! It's the very latest in modern kitchen technology."

"What does it do?" asked Yaakov.

"Oh, all sorts of things," explained Mr. Sapir, his voice sounding more patient now than a few minutes earlier. "That Kitchen Caesar Deluxe is a robotic kitchen controller and organizer. Whenever you want to eat a meal, or even a snack, all you have to do is tell the Kitchen Caesar Deluxe. It lowers itself from the ceiling, stretches out its arms, grabs food from the refrigerator, closes it, picks up utensils for spreading jelly and the like, and hands off those food items to the toaster, the stove, the microwave, the blender, or whatever device you need. Of course, the many kitchen appliances can automatically signal each other. They also communicate with the Kitchen Caesar Deluxe. But we're not really here to talk about that."

"Come, everyone," called Sabba Tzadok, from a small study attached to the other side of the kitchen, a room whose brown walls were lined with books and whose only furniture consisted of a desk and a chair. He seemed oblivious to all of the talk about the new kitchen device. "Now that you're here, I can explain what happened."

The Peretzes gathered around Sabba Tzadok, seated on a chair behind a wooden desk, and listened to him describing the events of June 8, 2025, the day that the pirates had broken into the Sapir family mansion.

"That robot dealer, Dilip Sitoop, was up on a ladder, busily installing that kitchen contraption, while I sat here looking over my old maps of Djerba. Djerba was once my home. In fact, I grew up praying in the big El-Ghriba synagogue, and have seen our family's ancient Torah scroll many times. Many people there still know how to make their own wines, and I brought my winemaking skills here to start our wineries. The grapes grow nicely here, and our wine has been quite flavorful. Anyway, my maps showed pictures of Djerba itself, the neighborhood around the synagogue, and the local geography around Djerba and Tunisia. There were a lot of notes on them too, including comments about the location of the ancient Torah scroll in El-Ghriba. When I started feeling tired, I got up to go to the living room and take a nap on that nice purple couch. After about ten minutes, I'd say, I suddenly heard some loud noises. There were crashing noises and the sounds of glass breaking, along with some screams. It was hard to hear what was being screamed, though. I got up and made my way to the kitchen as fast as these old legs could take me."

"You make a pretty good competition, Sabba," interjected Aharon.

Tzadok Sapir ignored the comment and continued. "I got there just in time to see six bizarre-looking thieves running from the basement door to the outside through the kitchen doorway. They were carrying that heavy box of family treasures with them. I also saw a trail of muddy footprints leading from a broken kitchen window to the study. A different set of footprints led from the study to another broken window in the kitchen. Broken glass from one window lay on the kitchen floor, evidence of a break-in. Broken glass from the other window lay outside in the garden, evidence that somebody had run outside by smashing his way out that window. Because the floors were muddied and both windows were broken even before the other pirates had managed to run outside, I reasoned that a seventh man had broken in through one window, grabbed my papers, and escaped through the other one, even before the jewels were stolen.

"Mr. Sitoop just stood on that ladder the whole time, staring into space with his mouth wide open.

"I hollered at him, 'What are you waiting for? Call the police already!'

"My shouting shocked him out of his daze. 'The police? Oh yeah,' he answered, kind of sluggishly. He came down from the ladder, picked up a phone and called, but it was too late for the police to do much. Sitoop and I saw the gang of six pirates running away to their van, jumping inside, and speeding down Paseo de Oro. Later, they turned and started heading southward, but eventually they disappeared from view."

"Did you get their license plate number?" asked Yehuda.

"I got part of it, but they were moving too fast for me," complained Sabba Tzadok. "Dilip Sitoop ran down to the street, jumped into his truck and started following them himself. But he couldn't catch up with them."

"He told us that he was able to see their treasure map," said Yehuda.

"Fine, so the treasure's been returned," continued Sabba Tzadok, "and we certainly appreciate it. But that's not the worst of what happened. The worst of it was that, when I checked my study again, my maps of Djerba were gone. The only other person here was Dilip Sitoop, and I doubt that he had any reason to take them. There's a seventh pirate on the loose who knows about the historic Torah scroll on Djerba. He hasn't turned up anywhere, and now there's nothing to stop him from going there and stealing it."

"Why would a pirate want a Torah scroll?" asked Yaakov. The story did not sit well with him. Was Dilip Sitoop really such an innocent, frightened bystander? Yaakov also began to feel a bit anxious. He hoped to get home soon enough to be able to pray the afternoon service, *Mincha*, with a *minyan*, a group of ten or more men. Still, it was hard to leave this house when an interesting story was so full of holes and his mind was so full of questions.

"Because of its age," explained Sabba Tzadok. "An ancient relic can be sold for a fortune these days, especially something known to be one of a kind. The oldest Torah scroll in the world, which has great value, as a useful religious item even today, would make its seller incredibly wealthy. Criminals have been hunting down and stealing artifacts from archaeological sites for many decades. This item from the ancient world just fell into its thief's lap."

Yaakov turned to Aharon Sapir. "But, Mr. Sapir, how did a whole gang of pirates even get into the house in the first place?" he pressed. "Don't you have a security system? All you had to do was push a button and a bunch of them came running outside a few seconds later."

"Yaakov, I don't think my grandfather could have reached that button on the wall in the front of the house in time," answered Aharon Sapir, patiently.

"Abba, I'm bored," complained Rachel.

"Me too," added Yosef. "Can we go home now?"

"Mr. Sapir," said Yehuda, addressing Aharon Sapir.

"Call me Aharon," he interrupted.

"Aharon," continued Yehuda, "I'm afraid we have to go. It's getting late. If we leave now, we can still make it back to Los Angeles before dark, in time to pray *Mincha* and put the kids to bed. Come, kids."

Yehuda Peretz led the way back toward the mansion's front door, with all three of his children and all three Sapirs following him.

Yaakov continued questioning Aharon Sapir as they walked. "Don't you have an automatic alarm system?" The entire crime, and the escape, simply sounded too easy to believe. "I mean, if you can afford a spidery robot for the kitchen, then why wouldn't you have an automatic system that calls the police as soon as a robber gets too close?"

"We do have an alarm system like that," explained Mr. Sapir. "We'd be foolish not to have one. But it was down at that moment. Mr. Sitoop had to shut off the electricity for a little while to install the robotic chef. At least that's what he told me he was going to do before he started. That Kitchen Caesar Deluxe involves all kinds of electrical wires and connections."

Mr. Sapir stopped walking, and turned to Yehuda with a serious expression. "Yehuda, how would you like to take your family on an all-expense-paid trip to Djerba? I hear that Djerba's nice this time of year. Isn't it, Sabba?"

Sabba Tzadok simply smiled and nodded.

"So, when you offered that to us outside, you were serious?" asked Yehuda, sounding a bit skeptical.

"That's right," answered Aharon Sapir. "Two weeks, on me. Tour the island, relax, explore El-Ghriba, and see if you can find out anything about that seventh pirate's whereabouts or plans. You won't have to stop him yourself. Just call the police if you see anything suspicious. As I said, all expenses paid. You can even fly there on my private jet. I'd go there myself, but Tamar and I are expecting a new baby Sapir any day now. We'd better stay here in Santa Barbara."

"It's a nice offer, Aharon," he answered, "and we'd certainly appreciate the rest, but I'd have to check with Leah first."

Yaakov felt his mind grasping at a solution to the mysterious robbery. He felt that he had almost figured it out, but just needed a bit more information. How could a bunch of scruffy pirates just walk up to a rich, expensive house in a fancy neighborhood, break in, steal a bunch of things, and then leave, especially when one of the witnesses saw everything happen? Why did they just ignore Mr. Sitoop, without harming him? Were they hoping to get caught?

It was time for Yaakov to speak up. "Abba, we'll never find that pirate. We don't even know what he looks like. We need some more information, and the only person who can help us is Mr. Sitoop. He was right there the whole time. He saw what Sabba Tzadok couldn't see, and heard all the shouts that Sabba Tzadok couldn't understand. I don't think we should go anywhere without talking to him first."

Yehuda looked at his eldest son. "You're turning into a real detective, aren't you, Yaakov? You're right. We won't even know who to look for until Dilip Sitoop tells us."

As they arrived at the mansion's front lobby, Yehuda's smartphone rang. "Hello?" he answered it. "Yes, Leah. How's the painting going? Oh, that's good news. I know it's been a long day. You'll never believe where we are, Leah. We're in Santa Barbara! Let me tell you what we're doing here."

He briefly told her about the exciting events of the past day and of Mr. Sapir's tempting offer of a free vacation. His conversation ended with the words, "Yaakov told me the same thing. Let's talk about it in the morning and go see Mr. Sitoop. We're about to leave, Leah. I'll try to make it home before eight."

The four Peretzes stepped outside and met AutoRiser, which had spent nearly an hour waiting outside for them. Yehuda exchanged contact information with Aharon Sapir.

"Thank you for your hospitality, Aharon," said Yehuda, shaking Aharon's hand. "Leah and I appreciate your offer, but I'm afraid we can't accept it just yet. We'll think about it and call you in the morning."

The children buckled themselves and AutoRiser into their seats in the family SUV. "Abba, I think we should find a new robot store," said Yaakov, sitting in the front seat, after Yehuda Peretz had started the engine and begun the long drive home. "There's something weird about Mr. Sitoop."

"I'll tell you what I told Mr. Sapir," replied Yehuda. "We'll think about it."

5 DILIP SITOOP REVEALS MORE

"Good morning to you, valued customers!" exclaimed the shiny robot greeter bolted to the sidewalk in front of Dilip Sitoop's store. To Yaakov, that robot greeter always looked quite ridiculous, like a glorified clown that he might have enjoyed at the age of four or five. By now, he was so used to it that he usually just ignored it. His mother and father stood behind the three children, all waiting for the store to open.

"Here we go again," groaned Yosef, rolling his eyes as the recorded message continued. "It was only funny the first five hundred times. Why can't Mr. Sitoop change that silly message more than once a decade?"

While Yosef ranted, Rachel mimicked the phony, bubbly voice, word for word: "I'm Siggy! Welcome to Sitoop Cybernetics, your one-stop shop for all your robotic needs. It's Monday morning. Why not start the day right with a healthy breakfast prepared specially for you by AutoGrubber? AutoGrubber provides orange juice, hot buttery toast and even scrambled eggs! For twenty-two extra cents a day – just a buck less than the price of a postage stamp – your orange juice comes fresh squeezed! Bread, eggs, oranges, and juice not included."

"You know, it does change from time to time, Yosef," explained Yaakov rather matter-of-factly. "At about twelve o'clock it plays the lunch version of the AutoGrubber message."

"Blah, blah, blah," replied Yosef. "AutoGrubber sounds even dumber than that Kitchen Caesar Deluxe we saw yesterday, just a little less expensive." He then turned to face his mother. "Imma, can't we just go home already? I'm tired of coming here."

Leah Peretz gave her son a stern look. She was a woman of average height, a down-to-Earth person with a no-nonsense attitude. Her only personal luxuries were the various flowery hats that she matched to her modest outfits, one hat for every day of the week. Of Yaakov's parents, his mother seemed to be the more practical one, serious and fairly strict without seeming cruel. She was a talented artist who didn't sound or act like one, except when she actually painted. She never seemed interested in made-up fantasy stories, fairy tales or make-believe. Faraway trips were just fine with her, if there was actually somewhere to go and something to do when she got there. She usually seemed to put up with her husband's sense of adventure; however, the one thing that seemed to upset her most was risking the children's safety, no matter how much "fun" was involved.

"We're not leaving until I've spoken to Mr. Sitoop," came Leah's blunt reply. "I've got a thing or two to say to that man." With those words, she pushed hard on the handle of the store's glass front door. The door didn't budge.

Suddenly, red lights began to flash, and loud siren-like noises blared from Siggy. Its mechanical voice delivered a new announcement. "The time is now 7:59 AM. Regular business hours are from 8:00 AM to 5:00 PM. Please return during those hours."

Leah's face took on a puzzled look. "I've never known Mr. Sitoop to be so uptight about 'regular business hours.' What's gotten into him?"

"That's what I want to find out, Imma," commented Yaakov. "Mr. Sapir's Sabba said that Mr. Sitoop acted kind of weird at their house."

"He probably spends too much time hanging around with robots and not enough time with people," offered Yosef, by way of explanation. "It's starting to get to him."

Leah pushed on the front door again, opening it, and led the family inside. *I know that look and that walk,* thought Yaakov. *She's charging in like a lioness. Somebody's in trouble.*

As he entered the store, Yaakov immediately noticed a timid-looking Dilip Sitoop, cowering in his little office chair behind the front counter. He just sat there and stared downward, arms hanging limply by his sides, not seeming to notice the customers who had just come inside. Over the years, Yaakov had come to expect the warm greetings that Dilip Sitoop normally delivered to the shoppers who visited his place of business. The man slumped into a black leather seat this morning was not the same Dilip Sitoop whose story Yaakov had gotten to know.

Dilip Sitoop was an ambitious man. He had

emigrated from India with his family five years earlier, after graduating at the top of his class at the Indian Institute of Science in Bangalore. Robots were his specialty, and he had won a number of awards for his creative inventions. After finishing school, Dilip went into the robot business. He soon discovered, to his dismay, that not many people in his home country were able to afford his human-shaped inventions. Dilip therefore brought his wife, Birla, and their two young children, Shamtar and Madhur, to America to strike their fortune. He figured that an expensive city like Los Angeles must be filled with people who craved human-like assistants that never went on strike or complained about the air conditioning. By now, Yaakov was quite familiar with Dilip Sitoop's story. On most visits to Sitoop Cybernetics, Dilip greeted Yaakov and his family with an eager smile and another tale about his youth in India. Today, however, was different. Mr. Sitoop wore a worried expression, and seemed very defeated.

Yaakov's parents marched toward the counter and faced Mr. Sitoop. Leah immediately addressed him in a loud, irritated voice. "You, sir, are in big trouble. Our three children were put in harm's way because of your bumbling."

"Oh. . .hi," he answered feebly, sounding unusually shy. "Did you, uh, find that treasure?"

"Yes, we did," replied Yehuda, in a firm voice. "It's now safely back in Aharon Sapir's basement. But returning it was no simple task."

"Right," said Dilip Sitoop, timidly, his accent sounding a bit thicker than usual. "I guess it's a long drive, huh?"

Yehuda leaned forward and rested his elbows on the counter, staring the other man in the face. He addressed Mr. Sitoop slowly, in a low voice, with a seriousness that Yaakov had almost never heard before. To be in trouble with both Imma and Abba was very bad news, indeed. "We ran into a little obstacle when we tried returning that treasure chest, *Dilip*. Pirates. Six of them gathered around us on the Sapir mansion's front lawn and threatened us. Three young children had to stand helplessly and listen to threats from a filthy pirate, because you were too scared to return a lost treasure right away. You knew where it was, and could have taken care of it yourself, but you waited around for someone else to deal with the problem. Pirates think nothing of harming anybody, at any age. Those thugs are sitting in jail now, thank God, but there was another pirate, wasn't there? He managed to flee on the day of the robbery, and we think he's on the way to harm an unsuspecting Jewish community. We need your help to find him and stop him. After what we went through yesterday, I think you owe us."

Mr. Sitoop sat up a little bit straighter in his chair. "What community? What are you talking about? Anyway, what could I possibly do to help?"

Leah answered plainly. "You need to tell us whatever you know about that seventh pirate. You were right there in the Sapirs' kitchen, and you saw everything. That's what you can do to help us, and you'd better cooperate. Now, how much do you remember?"

Mr. Sitoop let out a sigh, and began speaking in a shaking voice. "Well, let's see now. There I was in the kitchen, installing a Kitchen Caesar Deluxe system. I had to stand on a ladder, you know, to connect it to the ceiling. All of a sudden, a whole gang of pirates broke into the kitchen. They just burst right in through the door while I was standing there. It was quite a shock. A whole group of them ran straight down to the basement, and then came back up the stairs carrying that big box of jewels you found. But one of those men left the group and headed for the study on the other side of the kitchen. He came right out of there carrying some rolled-up papers. That man escaped through the kitchen window. That's about all I remember, guys."

Questions flooded Yaakov's mind. That story was a lot different from Sabba Tzadok's version, and Yaakov couldn't contain himself. "Mr. Sitoop, what you mean by 'one of those men separated from the group?' We were in that house yesterday, and Tzadok Sapir told us that the seventh pirate broke into the house through one window and out through another window. He was already gone even before the other six ran away with the stolen treasure box."

"Oh, was that how it happened?" asked Mr. Sitoop. "Well, I guess it could have happened that way. It's all so hard to remember. It was a few weeks ago already, and I was really panicked by the whole thing. Have they fixed those windows yet?"

"The windows are fine now," answered Yaakov, flatly. He was still bothered by Mr. Sitoop's story. "But how could that pirate have known to run straight to the study? He couldn't have seen what was on the desk when he broke in, and even if he did, he would have just seen some papers. My father told me how primitive most pirates are. That man probably can't even spell. Why would he want to run over to a desk, snatch up some maps of Djerba, and leave?"

Mr. Sitoop seemed a little bit bothered by the question. "I don't know," he said, quickly. "Maybe he saw some pretty pictures on them. Maybe he thought they were ads for rum. What difference does it make?"

Yaakov ignored the question, but fired back another of his own. "Why didn't you call the police right away, Mr. Sitoop? Why did you wait for the pirates to escape first?"

Dilip Sitoop stood up to his full height and stared down at Yaakov. Yaakov didn't blink. "Kid," said Mr. Sitoop, in an annoyed and insulting tone, "don't you know how to listen? I told you I was in a state of shock. I didn't know what to do. I couldn't do anything. I'd like to see how you behave in that kind of situation."

"Mr. Sitoop," replied Yaakov calmly and boldly, "don't you think it's odd that a bunch of pirates knew how to find the kitchen from outside an enormous mansion that they'd never been in before? You really can't tell where anything is just by looking at the outside of that huge house. And there's more than one kitchen, so how did they figure out which one. . ."

"Get out of my store!" exclaimed Dilip Sitoop, interrupting Yaakov's question. "All of you! In fact, if you're not out of here in thirty seconds, I'll get my security robots to help you find the door!"

"How dare you talk to my son that way!" shouted Leah, stepping forward.

Dilip exploded. "How dare you people come in here and start pestering me with insulting questions! That crime had nothing to with me!"

Yaakov had never seen Mr. Sitoop speak or behave this way before. He was used to seeing a much calmer robot dealer, with a pleasant and welcoming personality. By acting so enraged, the usually mild man now made Yaakov's suspicions seem true. Dilip Sitoop had to be guilty of something, and was obviously trying to hide it. Yaakov didn't know yet what that something was, but he began forming an idea to help discover what it was.

Dilip reached under the counter for a moment, apparently pressing a button. Instantly, two of the store's walls opened, each one revealing a secret chamber. Four tall, red, scary-looking robots stood in each chamber. These androids were taller than any of the robots that the Peretzes owned. In fact, they were taller than any robot that Yaakov had ever seen. Each one had beady, snake-like eyes and long, thick arms and legs. At the end of each arm was a menacing metal claw of a hand. The robots began walking quickly out of their chambers as soon as the doors opened. Soon, the Peretzes found themselves boxed in by eight security robots.

The robot closest to the front door extended its left arm and pointed toward the door. It aimed its gaze at Leah and Yehuda. "The exit is this way, sir," said its artificial voice.

"Wait a minute," said Yehuda, "we're not done yet." He tried to approach Mr. Sitoop again by walking past one of the robots, but it stood in his way and held up a mechanical palm.

"Just go that way, sir," it said, pointing toward the front door with its other arm.

Rachel held onto her mother and began whimpering. "Imma, let's get out of here. I'm afraid of those things," she said, almost crying.

Yaakov knew that this visit to Mr. Sitoop was his only chance to learn any information about the mysterious seventh pirate. He couldn't allow his family to be thrown out of the store. If they left now, they would never be let back inside, and Mr. Sitoop would never talk to them again. It was time to say something.

"Mr. Sitoop," yelled Yaakov, "I'm warning you! If that seventh pirate makes his way all the way to Djerba and robs the Jewish community, the police will start asking questions. They'll want to find out how, when and where the pirate got his information. Since you were in the house when he stole those maps, the police will start pointing fingers at you. You'd better have a good story for them. So far, even I figured out that whatever you said didn't make sense."

"I told you that you were in trouble, Dilip," added Leah. "Your problems are about to get worse. Remember the International Robotics Convention? There are rules about the kinds of robots you're allowed to have. Security robots are illegal! You can be arrested just for owning those things. . .or maybe not. Still don't want to cooperate?"

"No! Please don't report me!" shouted Dilip Sitoop in a panicked voice. "Okay, I won't throw you out," he added nervously. "Security, go back to your rooms."

Each red robot said, "Have a nice day." Then, all eight of them walked back into their hidden chambers. Mr. Sitoop pressed a button, and the doors to the hidden chambers closed. He then sat down, buried his face in his hands and began to cry.

"I made a big mistake," he managed to say between sobs. "I'm sorry." He lifted his head, faced all five Peretzes and continued slowly. "There's more to the story than I told you before. Business hasn't been so good lately. You see for yourselves that there are no other customers here. There's too much competition from the big robot sellers that are getting bigger every day, like Cyborg World and Andy's Androids. So a few weeks ago, when I was in Santa Barbara on my way to the Sapir home to install their new Kitchen Caesar Deluxe, an ugly brown van pulled up next to my truck while I was stopped at a red light. A sloppy-looking man in a red and white striped shirt yelled out the window, 'Hey, are you on your way up to that big fancy house?'

"'Yes,' I said. 'Why do you want to know?'

"'Find us a way in there and we'll pay you good! Real good! We promise.' He was just one of the pirates in that gang. The rest of them were piled into the back of the brown van, or so I imagined.

"It was a really tempting offer. What could I do? I was having trouble even paying my bills, and I'd already had to fire some of my workers. So I figured I'd just find an easy way for the pirates to grab something quickly and leave. Since I was going into the Sapirs' house anyway to install a major electronic device, I could say that I needed to shut off the electricity for about twenty minutes. That way, the alarm system wouldn't work. Then, I'd quietly call the pirate gang with my little cell phone, tell them how to find something valuable, and pretend to be shocked by the whole thing until they left. When Mr. Sapir's grandfather left his study to take a nap, I snooped around a bit. I saw the maps of Djerba with notes about the world's oldest Torah scroll, and realized that it was probably worth a fortune. But they wouldn't be able to get it if the police were on their trail. So I also set up a distraction: some of them would grab an expensive item and run away with it, and the police would chase them, while another pirate or two grabbed the map to the *really* valuable artifact. One bunch of pirates would be chased by the police, and maybe even caught, but the other one or two of them would get away with a massive heist. The police wouldn't even know to look for the runaways. And, Pete Weasel probably figured that he could just use his new treasure to bribe the other pirates out of prison later, if he needed them.

"Pete Weasel and his gang followed me to the house. They stayed in their van, parked by the sidewalk, while I went inside. I secretly called Pete Weasel and told him quickly about the maps of Djerba. I told him I'd also discovered the basement, where that treasure chest lay, and he thanked me for accidentally finding the thing he wanted to steal. Then, I told Pete that he only had a short time to get in before I turned the alarm system back on, and that I'd send an immediate signal to the police while he was still inside if he or any of his men tried to harm me.

"After the whole incident, I felt really guilty, so I followed the pirates as far as I could. On their way out of the city, one of them gleefully held up a desert map and drew a big, red 'X' on it. I quickly took a picture of it and then turned around and headed the other way."

Mr. Sitoop looked at the Peretzes and held out his empty hands like a beggar. To Yaakov, he resembled a hunted rabbit just cornered by a pack of wolves. He had a look of failure and defeat. "Please, please, don't turn me in!" he begged in a whiny, miserable voice. "I've tried to be good and honest for my whole life, but things were really getting tough and I didn't know what else to do! I only messed up this one time. It was just *one mistake*! Could you please give me another chance?"

Yehuda looked at him sternly. "How could you be so foolish?" he asked. "Did you really expect those pirates to give you any of the riches they promised you? They'll never pay you a penny, and you're actually lucky they won't. I'm surprised you're still alive! The only person who can give you another chance is Mr. Sapir. We'll let you off the hook on two conditions: Mr. Sapir has to forgive you for helping those pirates break into his house, and you need to tell us everything – and I mean *everything* – that you know about the missing seventh pirate."

"Oh, and one more thing," added Leah. "Get rid of those security robots. We can prove that you have them. Can't we, Yaakov?"

"Sure we can!" answered Yaakov, holding up a tiny digital camera that displayed a picture of Mr. Sitoop's tall electronic thugs. In the background, the words "Sitoop Cybernetics," painted on the outside of the store's glass doors, could be read backwards. Shadows of those words were projected onto the carpet in at the store's entrance.

"Okay, okay, I'll do whatever you say," said Mr. Sitoop, letting out another sigh. "I'll call Mr. Sapir right now, all right? Will that make you happy? Let me just get his number. . ." He picked up a small black cell phone and began examining it.

Yaakov no longer trusted Dilip Sitoop. *What if he just pretends to call Aharon Sapir and then gives us a made-up story about that pirate?* he wondered. He suspected that Mr. Sitoop might lie just to get the Peretzes off his back. Maybe Mr. Sitoop still, secretly, wanted that pirate to steal Djerba's ancient Torah scroll and to sell it for a fortune. Maybe he still hoped that the pirate on the loose would reward him. Yaakov had to speak up again.

"Mr. Sitoop," he said, boldly, before Dilip could dial any numbers, "my parents really shouldn't let you go so easily. I think they need proof that you're actually talking to Mr. Sapir and not just calling up the time while you pretend to apologize. In fact, I don't think they should believe you unless Aharon Sapir's grandfather is there too."

"What are you talking about?" asked Mr. Sitoop, scornfully. "You want me to go all the way back to Santa Barbara to talk to them in person?"

"No," replied Yaakov. "I want you to talk to all three Sapirs – Aharon, Tamar and Tzadok – on a video conference call from our house. That way, all of us know that you're doing what you say and telling the truth. You won't be able to lie in front of Tzadok Sapir, because he remembers the facts better than you do."

"That's a fine idea, Yaakov," said Leah, with a smile. "Let's go."

"What, now?" asked Mr. Sitoop in disbelief. "But I can't just close up my store so early in the morning!"

"What's the problem?" asked Yaakov, casually. "Call it an early lunch break. Call it a breakfast break. You can even have Siggy announce it. You need to change that greeting message, anyway."

6 HOT ON THE PIRATE'S TRACKS

"Now remember, kids, no funny faces," warned Yehuda Peretz, as his family gathered around the large video conferencing screen that occupied most of one living room wall. It was controlled by an electronic keypad attached to another wall. They were joined by Mr. Sitoop, who slumped sheepishly into an armchair. The children stood to his left, and their parents to his right. Yaakov held his digital camera discreetly behind his back, in his left hand. I have to be prepared, he told himself, in case this crook tries anything funny.

Yehuda pushed some buttons on the keypad, causing the screen to come to life. Within seconds, Aharon, Tamar and Tzadok Sapir appeared on the screen. The three of them sat on a sofa in a room that Yaakov did not recognize, Aharon in the middle and the others on either side of him. It looked like a cozy den in a section of the Sapir mansion that the Peretzes had not seen during yesterday's visit. A potted plant stood at each side of the sofa, and hazy sunlight shone onto the den's rug from a medium-sized window. Sabba Tzadok ignored the conference call as he peered into a small book, diligently studying its words of ancient wisdom. From the place where Yaakov stood, it appeared to be a volume of the Talmud.

Aharon Sapir was the first to speak. "Hello, Yehuda. Good morning. You've got quite a group there with you. I even see Dilip. And is that the misses?"

"Yes," answered Leah, with a smile. "Leah Peretz. It's nice to finally meet you."

"Likewise. I'm Aharon Sapir," replied Aharon. "Next to me are my wife, Tamar, and my grandfather, whom we call 'Sabba Tzadok.' You have a lovely bunch, as we discovered yesterday. Now what can I do for you? Have you thought about my offer?"

"We've thought about it," answered Leah, "but we can't accept it yet. Not until Mr. Sitoop speaks to you. He has something important to say." She then looked down at Mr. Sitoop. "Don't you?"

"Yeah," said Dilip Sitoop, with hesitation. He squirmed in his seat before adding, "I've got something to say about. . .robots."

"Oh?" asked Tamar. "What is it, a new Kitchen Caesar Deluxe upgrade? So soon?"

"Well, not really," he answered, nervously. "I mean. . ." His voice drifted off to silence, and he started looking at his shoes.

Yaakov quickly shoved his digital camera in front of Dilip Sitoop's face, showing him the picture of his security robots that he had taken less than half an hour ago. "Remember what you had to tell Mr. Sapir? It was very important. . .right?"

"Right," said Dilip Sitoop, letting out a sigh. "Okay,

Aharon, are you ready to listen?"

"Yes," responded Aharon, patiently.

"Okay," continued Mr. Sitoop, slowly. "Here's what happened. I was the one responsible for the break-in at your house a few weeks ago."

"What?" asked Mr. and Mrs. Sapir together, in shocked voices. Both of them sat up straight, while Sabba Tzadok simply continued studying.

"I'm very, very sorry," continued Dilip, "but I was responsible for the whole thing. What could I do? What can I say? Things were going very badly for me at the time, and still are. I've been losing customers right and left. I tried everything I could think of to drum up more business – more ads, more discounts, but nothing seemed to work. On that day, I was coming to your house to install your Kitchen Caesar Deluxe, and that bunch of pirates pulled up right next to me and started talking to me from their van. They offered to reward me if I could find a way for them to get inside and steal something valuable. So, I, uh. . .started looking around the house. I found out where you kept your fancy jewels, and saw those maps to the antique scroll on the faraway island. Then, I called the pirates and told that them they had to make it quick – just a fast break-in, a simple burglary, and then they had to get out of there right away. I think you know the rest."

"Dilip Sitoop," said Aharon, slowly leaning forward, "you ought to be ashamed of yourself. Look at all the damage that you caused! What were you thinking? You didn't have to resort to crime to improve your lot! I would have been happy to help you! All you had to do was ask. Do you have any idea how many rich wine experts we get as customers? Many of them would love your advanced robots."

"Sure," said Yosef. "You know, there's an old saying: 'A fool and his money are soon parted.' A rich fool would surely love to waste a fortune on some robots."

Yaakov finally saw his chance to find out who this mysterious seventh pirate was. "Mr. Sapir, right now, you have something that Mr. Sitoop wants, and he has something that all of us want."

"What can Dilip Sitoop offer us?" asked Aharon.

"Information about the escaped pirate," responded Yaakov, glaring at the nervous robot dealer, "that seventh one who's still on the loose." I'm going to hunt down that pirate and find him, he thought, and there's nothing you can do to stop me. He looked up at Mr. Sapir and continued. "Would you be willing to forgive Mr. Sitoop if he helps us find out where that seventh pirate is? We can't stop him if we can't find him, and I think Mr. Sitoop has learned his lesson."

"I suppose I can forgive you, Dilip," answered Aharon Sapir, plainly, "knowing that you were so down on your luck. I guess it was easy to be tempted, and I don't know what I'd do if I were in your shoes. But only if you really help us. Now tell us whatever you know about that pirate. Everything."

Dilip sat up and looked straight ahead. He let out a breath. "Let's see now. I remember seeing a bunch of bizarre-looking ruffians break in through the back kitchen door. At about the same time, another one came crashing in through the kitchen window. He wore thick gloves to protect his hands, a red and white checkered shirt and ripped blue jeans. He was a tall, overgrown, sloppy character. One of the men who broke in through the doorway, a bearded guy who seemed to be the leader of the bunch, yelled a command at the one from the window. It was something like, 'Bobby the Brute, go grab the papers and high-tail it back to the ranch!' The sloppy pirate grabbed some papers from the desk and then smashed his way out through the other window."

An image of Pete Weasel came to mind as soon as Yaakov heard Mr. Sitoop's description.

"I wonder what he meant by 'the ranch,'" said Yehuda. "It's a slang term for 'home.' Could Pete Weasel have been talking about to a base of some sort?"

"Maybe there's a big pirate house where a bunch of them live," suggested Rachel. "If we look around for a while we can find it and catch that pirate!"

Yaakov spoke down to her in an authoritative voice. "Rachel, pirates live on ships, not in houses."

"These pirates were living in a little cave on Anacapa Island," retorted Aharon, "or so they claimed when my security guards interrogated them. They also identified their ship, and the Santa Barbara Port Authority impounded it. Last night, I checked with the Port Authority and found out that the ship has been sitting there at the dock for the past few weeks. So Bobby the Brute hasn't taken any trips, and now that his ship's been impounded, he isn't going far."

"Then there's nothing to worry about," said Leah. "He must be wandering around somewhere by himself. I guess we won't be taking that trip to Djerba after all, but we certainly appreciate your offer, Mr. Sapir. Have a very nice day."

"Imma, please don't hang up yet!" shouted Yaakov

as he turned around and faced his mother. Pete Weasel had given him an important clue through Dilip Sitoop. If pirates spent most of their time living on ships, and Bobby the Brute was supposed to run back to his "ranch" with Sabba Tzadok's maps, then maybe there was still some reason to worry. Anyway, didn't Aharon Sapir say that Pete Weasel's pirate gang circled around the bay in little boats, keeping their eyes on his family treasures, a week or two before the robbery? Perhaps a small vessel could go rather far after all, if one tried hard enough.

"Yaakov, we have things to do today," came Leah's stern reply. "Abba needs to open the store in fifteen minutes, you and your siblings have to go to camp, and I've got more artwork to finish. Dilip over here has to get rid of some. . .*scrap metal*. . .don't you, Dilip?"

Yaakov spoke quickly before Dilip could answer the cynical question. "Please, Imma, I think I'm onto something. Could you please give me five minutes to figure something out before you hang up? Please?"

"All right, you have five minutes. Not a second more."

"Thanks, Imma," he called, rushing out of the living room, down the hallway and out the door to the backyard. He ran straight to the garage door, opened it, dashed inside, and quickly approached the sixth robot in the family's lineup: Buzzing Bill. Reaching behind the tall robot with his right hand, he found and flicked its power switch. Then, he watched for a few seconds as Buzzing Bill came to life.

Of all the Peretz family's robots, Buzzing Bill looked and sounded least like a real person. Yaakov figured that the robot's human-like nickname was meant to make up for all that it lacked in human appearance and voice. Buzzing Bill was designed and built for sending and receiving electromagnetic communication signals. His parents never allowed him to do anything illegal with Buzzing Bill, like listening in on other people's private walkie-talkie conversations or eavesdropping on paid broadcasts, but Yaakov was well aware of the legal, public information made available by satellites. In fact, Buzzing Bill was constructed with a small satellite dish on its head. Yaakov needed a wide-area, real-time weather map, and he needed it right away. He led the robot out of the garage.

"Hey there," said a metallic voice from somewhere within Buzzing Bill, "what's the buzz?" This robot certainly had nothing resembling a mouth.

"Buzzing Bill," instructed Yaakov, "bring me a weather map showing the coast near Santa Barbara."

The satellite dish raised itself to a more vertical position, and rotated itself by about twenty or thirty degrees. A map showing the coastline just south of Santa Barbara appeared on Buzzing Bill's display screen. A small number of ships were visible, but it was impossible to tell who occupied any of them. Yaakov continued his search.

"Buzzing Bill," he commanded, "start reading any words or letters written on the boats or ships that are in the ocean right now. I'm looking for the word 'ranch': R-A-N-C-H."

"No ranch found," droned Buzzing Bill's metallic voice.

"Okay," said Yaakov, not yet ready to quit, "now expand your search. Keep searching those real-time maps of the Pacific Ocean for any boats or ships that say 'ranch.' Continue looking westward, but not north of Fresno or south of San Diego." The view on Buzzing Bill's screen began scrolling westward. "Keep going, Buzzing Bill. Look for the word 'ranch'. Now keep searching westward until I tell you to stop."

Before he knew it, Yaakov found himself staring at the image of a small fishing boat in the Mediterranean Sea with the words "RANCH DRESSING" painted on its roof. The boat was in a very different time zone, where clocks ran about ten hours ahead of Los Angeles time. At the end of June, the time difference meant that anyone on that fishing boat could watch a lovely sunset as Yaakov looked on from his backyard. As soon as he saw the boat, Yaakov let out a gasp. "Buzzing Bill, stop there!" he exclaimed. "Now track that boat. Keep tracking it. I'll be right back."

Yaakov turned around and raced back into the house, almost bumping into his father. "Everybody, come quick! Look what I found!" he yelled. "Hurry!"

His family, and Dilip Sitoop, came outside and gathered around Buzzing Bill's display screen. They watched the little boat that remained at the center of the screen as it moved forward. Yaakov pointed to the lettering painted on its side, and all agreed that they could read the words "RANCH DRESSING." The long shadows that trailed the tiny vessel were a sure sign that it was heading westward, quite possibly toward Djerba.

"Buzzing Bill, zoom in on the boat, as closely as you can," commanded Yaakov.

His parents' jaws dropped as the image of the boat grew larger and larger, until everybody in the yard could identify a man standing on it. He wore the same raggedy outfit that Dilip Sitoop had described in his account to Aharon Sapir. His face was now somewhat bearded and rather filthy, after several weeks of obvious neglect. In his left hand he held a raw fish that he waved in front of his nose, seeming to smell it.

"That's him!" cried Dilip. "That's Bobby the Brute! He made it halfway around the world in a fishing boat! He'll reach Djerba before we know it! What are we gonna do?"

Yaakov turned to his mother. "How does that free vacation sound now, Imma?"

7 A CLUE ON THE BEACH

The view was magnificent. It was the type of scene that Yaakov's mother loved to paint, a *seascape*, as she called the stunning ocean views that hung on many walls of the Peretz home. From this window in their elegant suite at the Desert Star Resort, Yaakov had a direct view of Djerba's northern shoreline. The Desert Star was possibly the most comfortable and convenient hotel that Mr. Sapir could have chosen for them, located about 20 minutes from the airport, and close enough to the beach to give grand ocean views. In addition, thanks to the many Jewish vacationers who flocked to Djerba from Israel and elsewhere to visit historical sites like the El-Ghriba synagogue, the Desert Star offered a fine selection of kosher cuisine.

Yaakov sat on a cushioned chair and stared at the Mediterranean Sea. Many miles of calm, blue ocean water stretched to the horizon, shimmering in the early Thursday morning sunlight. Gentle waves crashed against the sandy beach. Soon, that beach would be bustling with the European and Israeli tourists who often visited Djerba at this time of year, but Yaakov could still savor a moment or two of quiet thought before his family awoke. After two hectic days of packing, planning, hurrying to Santa Barbara to meet Mr. Sapir's pilot, and flying to the other side of the world, Yaakov couldn't blame his parents and siblings for being exhausted.

Still, Yaakov had felt too jumpy to sleep late that morning. He had leapt boldly out of bed shortly after five-thirty, like a hunter anxious to catch his prey. The day before, his mother had reminded all three children that they were in Djerba mainly to enjoy a nice and relaxing vacation, but Yaakov couldn't get his mind off of the pirate chase. We're coming for you, Bobby the Brute, he thought, staring at the vast Mediterranean Sea. You crossed oceans to rob the Jewish People of something worth more than its value in money. You won't get away with it. Yaakov felt unstoppable.

"Good morning, Mr. Early Bird!" came his mother's voice from behind, interrupting Yaakov's imagined pursuit of Bobby the Brute, filthy pirate. "How are the worms today?"

Yaakov jumped out of chair and turned around to face her. She was fully dressed, but seemed just a bit drowsy. "Good morning, Imma," he greeted her, smiling. "Worms aren't kosher, you know, but in some countries in this part of the world, Jews used to eat grasshoppers."

"Did they now?" she asked, sounding impressed with her son's knowledge. "What are you doing up so early? Go lie down and get some more rest!"

"I'm up to catch Bobby the Brute!" he announced,

proudly.

At that moment, Rachel and Yosef ran into the family room, followed by their father. The two children headed straight to the window and began to chatter about the scattered sailboats that they claimed they could see in the distance, and who was probably sailing on each one. Leah approached them and joined their game of imagination.

"So here's my big pirate hunter!" declared Yehuda, rubbing Yaakov's yarmulke and hair. "Eleven years old and he's already chasing down outlaws. Yaakov, I'm going to try to find the nearest synagogue for *Shacharit*. Do you want to come with me?"

"No thanks, Abba, I already prayed *Shacharit* right after I got up." Though Yaakov sometimes did like to go with his father to the synagogue for *Shacharit*, the traditional Morning Prayer, today was a different sort of day. A wicked pirate was on the loose, and Yaakov couldn't wait to run outside and nab him. Nothing could stand in his way.

"All right," answered Yehuda, in his usual patient and cheerful style. He then turned to his wife. "Leah, I'll try to be back by about eight. There are about a dozen synagogues in Hara Kebira, nearby, so it shouldn't be hard to find one."

Leah turned away from the window and faced her husband. "Take your time, Yehuda. We might not even be here when you come back. I thought today would be a great day to take the kids to that beach. Look out the window. There's nobody there. When else do we get a whole beach to ourselves?"

"Yeah!" cried Yosef and Rachel excitedly.

"Have fun," said Yehuda, as he turned to leave.

"We'll go as soon as you kids are ready," added Leah. "How about some breakfast?"

"Great idea, Imma," said Yaakov. Though anxious to run outside and start looking for clues to Bobby the Brute's whereabouts, Yaakov was also hungry. Also, breakfast was another chance to take advantage of his very own robotic creation: Digital Drudge. Digital Drudge was Yaakov's personal assistant. It was only slightly taller than Yaakov, and a bit faster than some of the Peretzes' other robots. It had taken Yaakov over a year to build, and two months to program, Digital Drudge. By now, this machine could serve snacks and meals, wash dishes, put away shoes, bring slippers, make beds, find missing toothbrushes, and carry school supplies down steps or along sidewalks. Yaakov was very proud of his invention.

"Digital Drudge is here to serve us," declared Yaakov, proudly. "Breakfast for four coming right up!" He ran into the bedroom of the family suite and briskly approached a robot leaning against the wall closest to his bed. "Digital Drudge, bring a pitcher of orange juice, four cups and a package of cookies to the balcony. Put all those things on the table."

"Service with a smile," answered Digital Drudge in a metal voice, repeating yet again the phrase that had become a common quote in the Peretz home lately. The robot slowly walked over to the little refrigerator that stood against another wall, opened it, took out a pitcher of juice, and placed it on a little tray. Then, it picked up four drinking glasses provided by the hotel and added each one. Digital Drudge then lifted the tray with both hands, and made its way to the family room. Yaakov sat on a comfortable chair and eagerly waited for Digital

Drudge to arrive.

"Look at that slow-moving piece of junk," remarked Yosef. "Even when we're on vacation he has to bring those things."

"I think Digital Drudge is kind of funny," said Rachel, with a chuckle. "Look how it walks. It keeps its arms and legs so stiff!"

"I don't think it's funny," replied Yosef, making an annoyed face as the robot began placing glasses on the table. "I think it's dumb. We could have drunk a few glasses of juice by now."

"Those *things* may come in very handy, Yosef," said Yaakov, feeling offended by his brother's lack of appreciation for robots. "You never know when we might need one."

"Yeah, right," answered Yosef. "What are we gonna do here with AutoShoveler and Tx-Rex-Mod?"

"We're looking for a pirate. Like I said, you never know." Yaakov was happy to have those two robots around. They made him feel secure, like a confident carpenter who had to bring his most trusty power drill on every job. AutoShoveler had helped the family foil most of Pete Weasel's pirate gang, Yaakov reasoned, by helping them find that stolen treasure in the desert. Tx-Rex-Mod was designed and built for remote sensing. It could detect infrared waves, and could use radar waves, to find objects and spaces far away, even things buried underground. Since Pete Weasel's gang liked to dig, Yaakov imagined using Tx-Rex-Mod to find something buried very deeply underground and AutoShoveler to dig down and find it. To Yaakov, Bobby the Brute didn't exactly seem to be sharpest knife in the drawer, but maybe he had come up with a clever way around AutoShoveler's metal detector. Torah scrolls are made of parchment and wood, not metal.

Leah stepped in to break up the fight. "All right, kids, stop arguing. Yaakov, thank you for using your robot to bring us the juice and cookies. Yosef, if you don't want the robot to serve you, then get up and take some for yourself. Let's have a quick bite now and then head over to the beach before it gets crowded."

A short while later, Yaakov, Yosef, Rachel and their mother found themselves on smooth sand with beach toys, towels, and light sports equipment. As Yaakov had expected, Leah soon set up her easel with canvas and paint. She began to produce a picture of the nearby ocean scene. While she did so, the children began a game of volleyball. Since they had no volleyball net, Rachel and Yosef simply tried hitting the ball back and forth, over Yaakov's head. He actually found it quite amusing to be a volleyball net.

"This game is getting boring," said Rachel after about ten minutes. "I want to make something with the sand." She dropped the ball, turned around and picked up her bag of plastic pails, shovels and sieves that came in different shapes, sizes and colors. She started digging holes and filling buckets. The two boys continued playing without her, hitting the ball back and forth over a line in the sand that served as their net.

"Hey, look over there! I see something far away!" cried Rachel several moments later.

"What is it?" asked Yaakov, feeling slightly bothered by the interruption. He had actually taken his mind off the pirate and begun to enjoy the game.

"That thing over there!" Rachel pointed toward a

point farther down the beach. Yaakov followed his sister's finger, and spotted a brownish object that apparently had washed onto the shore.

"I don't know, Rachel," he answered. "Maybe it's a big box of bananas or something. Maybe it's garbage. Who cares?"

"I do! I want to see what it is!" Rachel started running toward the strange object.

"Boys, go follow your sister!" called Leah from behind her canvas. "See what she's doing! I'll catch up with you in a minute."

What in the world is Rachel up to? wondered Yaakov as he ran clumsily across the soft sand, alongside his brother. He wanted this trip to the beach to be over and done quickly, so that he could spend the rest of the day hunting for Bobby the Brute. Instead of chasing down a pirate, he was now pursuing his annoying little sister!

Eventually, the whole group reached the mysterious object. It was a small boat that had recently shipwrecked, striking the ground hard as it landed. Because there was no place nearby for the boat to dock, its pilot had apparently crashed the boat into the shore. Broken boards and a large hole in the front of the boat made it clear that it had not landed normally.

"Imma, can we climb on it?" asked Yosef, excitedly.

"Please?" added Rachel.

"No, kids," she replied, "just stay away from it. Let's go back now, pick up our stuff, and go back to the hotel."

The two youngest children started to plea with their mother for permission to explore the damaged vessel, but a large wave soon crashed over the boat, forcing them to run further from the shore for cover. After a few brief complaints, Rachel and Yosef followed their mother down the beach.

Yaakov trailed behind his younger siblings. He took several steps, and then felt something hit his left foot. Looking down, Yaakov saw a wooden board from the boat. At first, he thought nothing of it, but as he lifted his head, he noticed some black paint on the board. He squatted for a closer look at the paint marks. They seemed to be fragments of letters. He turned around for another look at the boat, and spotted several more painted boards that had broken off of it and now lay scattered in the wet sand by the shore. His mind began racing with possibilities. Could he have stumbled onto something important? He had to get his mother to turn around and examine this discovery before she and her younger children got too far away.

"Imma, look what I found!" he called to his mother. "Could you please come here?"

She turned around and began walking toward Yaakov in quick steps, with Yosef and Rachel following.

"Imma, look at these boards," said Yaakov, as soon as his mother arrived. "There were letters painted across them. Can you please help me put them back together?"

The four of them began to pick up the boat's boards, to carry them far away from the shore, and to arrange them on the dry sand. The three children made a game of using the paint marks to construct capital English letters, placing the loose boards next to each other to form whatever combination of words might be possible. When they were finished, Yaakov couldn't believe his eyes.

"Read that!" he gasped. "It says 'RANCH DRESSING'! Imma, we've found Bobby the Brute's boat. He's here on Djerba right now! I think we'd better go to the police."

"You're right, Yaakov," she answered, in a serious tone. "Let's go and meet Abba back at the hotel. From there, we'll drive over to the police station, together."

8 THE PIRATE'S PLOT

"We've just carried our playthings and my new painting from the beach. Okay, Yehuda, we'll meet you in front in five minutes. Drive safely. Bye." Leah ended her conversation with Yehuda, hung up her smartphone and placed it into her handbag. She then led the children out to the entrance of the Desert Star.

Yehuda Peretz soon arrived in a large, green rented minivan, which he parked in front of the curb where Yaakov and his siblings stood with their mother. To Yaakov, Djerba had a primitive feel. Since their arrival, Yaakov had not noticed any vehicles that drove themselves, and they all seemed to run on gasoline rather than chargeable electric batteries or solar power. There didn't seem to be many robots around here, either, and Yaakov's digital helpers had aroused some curious stares from the hotel staff. Yehuda climbed out of the minivan and began helping the others to load the wooden boards from Bobby the Brute's fishing boat into the trunk. As he approached the back of the minivan, Yaakov noticed an old-fashioned part extending from underneath it: a metal exhaust pipe. No matter, he thought. *The air is still nice and clean here, anyway.*

It was a short drive to the nearest police station. Police guarded the entrance to the Hara Kebira neighborhood, just a few miles from the Desert Star in Houmt Souk. This neighborhood had been attacked by foreign terrorists a little over twenty years previously, and had received extra security protection ever since then. Bobby the Brute's target, the El-Ghriba synagogue, was in a different neighborhood, Hara Seghira, about four miles away. Yaakov wondered if the security around El-Ghriba was tight enough to keep out that pirate. *Maybe there's nothing for us to do,* he thought, as they pulled up to a simple building with the word "Police" painted on its outside in English, French and Arabic.

"We're here, kids," announced Leah. "Everybody help carry in these wooden boards."

Inside, the Peretzes found a modest room where two stern-looking, uniformed officers sat behind a long wooden desk. On the right sat a large man with an imposing figure and an overgrown mustache. He wore a name badge that read "VALJEAN." The officer on the left was a shorter and skinnier fellow who wore the name "GASTON" on his nametag. Valjean looked up from the stack of papers in front of him and said something gruff to the group, in a language that sounded to Yaakov like French.

"We speak English," answered Yehuda. "We're Americans."

The officers looked at each other for a moment and

exchanged a few muttered phrases. Then, Gaston looked directly at Yehuda. "Are all those yours?" he asked, in a snobby-sounding tone, with a heavy French accent. "Those boards, I mean," he added after a few seconds. "They're filthy! Take them out of here!"

"Officer, we have to show you these," said Yaakov, trying to sound polite. "They're from a pirate ship! I mean, a pirate boat."

"Take your toy boats outside and play somewhere else." Officer Gaston dismissed them with an impatient wave of his hand.

"Please let me explain, officer," said Yehuda. "My wife and children found these boards on the beach. They came off a pirate's fishing boat. We have good reason to believe that the El-Ghriba synagogue is about to be robbed by a pirate whom we tracked here, all the way from America."

Officer Gaston squinted at him. "What pirate?"

The children excitedly began telling the two police officers about the events of the past few days. They told of their treasure hunt in the desert, their encounter with Pete Weasel and his pirate gang, the story of Bobby the Brute and his threat to the El-Ghriba Torah scroll, Bobby the Brute's little boat named "Ranch Dressing," and their trip to Djerba to find him.

After staring at the Peretzes silently for about ten seconds, Officer Gaston grunted. He then added, "I'm getting Chief Sharif. Wait here." He got up from his chair and walked into a back room. A few minutes later, he returned with a large, somewhat overweight, middle-aged man whose nametag bore the name "SHARIF."

Chief Sharif approached the desk and stood between the two younger officers. "What is this about a pirate?" he asked in a Middle Eastern accent.

Yaakov briefly repeated the story of the family's pursuit of Bobby the Brute. When he finished, he and his siblings began spreading the pirate's wooden boards across the floor. Together, they lined the boards next to each other in order, spelling the name of the boat.

"Look at this," announced Yaakov, when they were done. "We spelled out the name of his boat. He's here on Djerba, and we have to stop him before it's too late."

"Kids," said Chief Sharif, gruffly, "there's nothing I can do. All I have are your story and some pieces of wood that you say came from a pirate's boat. So what? I can't go and look for him. I can't do anything, unless I know he's about to commit a crime. Did he send you, or anybody, any threatening letters? Did he make any mean phone calls? Let's say you're right and he's on Djerba. Maybe he's just taking a vacation, like you people. Has he tried anything since he got here?"

"No," answered Yaakov, feeling defeated. Still, he refused to quit. I can't give up now, thought Yaakov, not when we're so close to stopping that thief! "But we know he's here on Djerba right now!" he added, quickly. "He came to steal something! The maps of Djerba and El-Ghriba disappeared as soon as Bobby the Brute escaped from Mr. Sapir's mansion, and we saw him on his boat before we got here. Please help us."

Chief Sharif leaned forward and stared directly at Yaakov. "What didn't you understand about what I said before? All I have is your story. I can't even send a patrolman to guard the building, based on that."

"Thanks for your time, officer," said Leah, as she and her husband turned to leave. "Let's go, kids." She motioned for the children to follow. Yosef and Rachel walked behind their parents, but Yaakov lingered for a moment. An idea suddenly sprang to mind.

"Imma and Abba," he called, as his family reached the station's front door, "please wait a minute." His parents turned to face him.

"What is it, Yaakov?" asked Leah, sounding impatient. "We're leaving now. Come on."

"Imma, I have an idea. Maybe Mr. Sapir can help us. Does he have any relatives still living here on Djerba?"

"Why don't we ask him?" Yehuda pulled his smartphone out of his left pocket. "It's kind of late at night in Santa Barbara, but he might still be up." Before he could dial a number, Chief Sharif interrupted him.

"Hey, people, this isn't a public bus station! If you want to make phone calls, make them outside!"

The Peretzes left the police station, and Yaakov helped his father load the wooden boards into the back of the minivan. Then, Yaakov listened to his father converse by phone with Aharon Sapir, while Yosef and Rachel paced around the dusty sidewalk and talked to their mother.

"Yes, Aharon, the hotel is fine," said Yehuda. "Thank you very much. Listen, we've run into a problem trying to catch that pirate. He's here, all right. We've even found his boat to prove that. But the police aren't helping us. We're standing by the little police station right in front of Hara Kebira. It was the closest one to the Desert Star, and it's not too far from El-Ghriba, either. The police aren't doing anything special to guard your family's Torah scroll. They don't seem to believe that this pirate's about to strike. Maybe they just don't care. Or, maybe it's because we're foreigners. Do you know any locals who could possibly. . .convince them?"

Yehuda listened to Mr. Sapir for a few minutes, interjecting occasional questions such as "Really?" and "He is?" Finally, he ended the conversation with the words, "Thank you, Aharon. We'll wait right here and see what happens."

After hanging up, Yehuda looked at his family and smiled. "Our friend, Aharon Sapir, is related to Moshe Haddad, the mayor of Houmt Souk. He's the mayor's nephew. Mr. Sapir just offered to contact Chief Sharif and ...*remind* him how important that ancient Torah scroll is to his – and to the mayor's – family. The police may decide to do something to stop that pirate after all. Let's wait here a bit and see what. . ."

"Excuse me, mister!" Chief Sharif flung open the police station's front door and hurried outside. He quickly approached Yehuda. "Good, you're still here. Yes, we have to go and stop that pirate from robbing the house of worship. It's very, very important. Why don't you go to back to the beach where you found your evidence? I'll send an officer in a car to follow you."

Back at the beach, Officer Gaston asked the Peretzes to show him Bobby the Brute's little boat. Yaakov, Yosef and Rachel led the way, with their parents and the officer trailing behind them, Leah carrying her paint supplies and Yehuda carrying two bags of the children's beach toys.

The children raced down the shore toward the spot where the small, battered boat had been discovered less than an hour earlier. Yaakov remembered that place well. He hurried along the beach as quickly as his tired legs would take him. With each step, he struggled against the soft sand that slowed him and made him feel sluggish. He tried to picture, as clearly as possible, the area around the spot where the boat had landed. A large number of whitish-orange, spiral-shaped seashells had lain scattered on that part of the beach. Yaakov also recalled seeing many tangled pieces of seaweed in the wet sand next to the boat. In addition, he remembered an old, abandoned picnic basket that lay upside down about twenty feet away from Bobby the Brute's wreck. There were a few decorative little paper umbrellas, too, the kind that Yaakov had sometimes seen floating in adults' fancy drinks.

Eventually, with their parents and Officer Gaston following closely behind, the children found the muddy spot where they had discovered the Ranch Dressing earlier that morning. The familiar shells, seaweed and picnic garbage were still there, just as Yaakov remembered. However, when he arrived at Bobby the Brute's landing spot, Yaakov began to quiver, and started feeling sick to his stomach. He was unprepared for such a disappointment. The boat was gone.

"What?" exclaimed Yosef, angrily stamping his foot in the mud. "It was here! The boat was right here! We all saw it, didn't we, Imma?"

"Yes, dear," she answered, with a bit of surprised nervousness. She then looked at Officer Gaston. "Uh, officer, the kids and I were all here this morning, and there really was a boat here. We all saw it in this exact spot."

A look of irritation came over Officer Gaston's face.

"Officer," said Yehuda, "my wife and kids don't just make up stories. If they say they saw the pirate's boat here, you can believe that it really was here. It must have been moved since they found it. Maybe it was washed away."

"It was a pretty decent boat," added Leah. "Maybe somebody stole it."

"Yeah, right," replied Officer Gaston, his voice dripping with contempt. "You know what, people? Quit wasting my time with your silly, touristy fairy tales." He turned around and headed toward the parking lot.

Rachel looked up at her father. "What should we do, Abba? The boat disappeared!"

"I know what I want to do, Rachel. Let's make a sandcastle! We've been here for over half a day and I still haven't enjoyed this beach yet." Yehuda opened the bag of sand toys that he had carried from the minivan, sat down on a patch of dry sand, and started helping Rachel build a castle. Yosef stared at their creation for a moment and then joined them.

Leah gave Yaakov a look of sympathy. "It's disappointing, I know, dear. You really wanted to nab that pirate right away. Look, we're not far from the neighborhood of the big synagogue, and *we* know he made it here. Let's be on the lookout ourselves. By now, El-Ghriba's probably closed for the day, but tomorrow morning we can go there and warn everyone about Bobby the Brute's plan. There's nothing else we can do until then, short of patrolling the synagogue ourselves around the clock until something happens. So for now, let's just enjoy the beach before the crowds start arriving and it gets too hot." She set up her easel and paint set, and soon began adding to the ocean view that she had started earlier that day. Yaakov stood next to her quietly and watched her paint, while his father, brother and sister continued playing.

Yaakov stared at his mother's painting, concentrating on the scene that grew richer and more detailed by the minute. Eventually, his brother's familiar voice distracted him. "Imma, can I go exploring?"

Leah looked up from her canvas and answered Yosef. "Yes, but don't wander too far off. Stay where Abba can see you. Yaakov, why don't you go with him?"

"Okay, Imma," he answered, eager for something exciting to do. "Let's go, Yosef."

The two boys walked along the beach at a brisk pace, staying far enough away from the shore to avoid getting wet. Occasionally, Yaakov stared at the distant sea and squinted to try to make out the features of the ships and boats that he thought he saw. He also looked back from time to time to make sure that he could still see his parents and Rachel. After a while, the sandy coast began to turn rocky. The soft, level, sandy ground gradually rose until the boys found themselves climbing a rough, bumpy hill. Yosef pulled himself up, onto a tall rock overlooking the water about fifteen feet below him.

"Hey Yaakov, look down there!" exclaimed Yosef, pointing downward. "I wonder what that is!"

Yaakov joined his brother on the tall rock and looked down toward the ocean. He saw an amazing sight, a cave in the rock wall, mostly filled with water. Inside the sea cave, a large object seemed to be stuck. Holding carefully onto the rock with his left hand, he reached into his right pocket, pulled out his digital camera, turned it on, and aimed it toward the cave.

With his index finger, he pushed a button to turn on the camera's built-in telescopic lens feature. Then, he squinted with his right eye and stared into the camera with his left eye. "Yosef, I think we've just found the rest of Bobby the Brute's boat!"

"Can I see?" asked Yosef, excitedly.

"Sure!" Yaakov held the camera in front of Yosef's face.

"Wow! That does look just like his boat. And it looks like he left a piece of paper on it. It must be stuck to his little table with ketchup, or fish oil, or something. There are some words on it."

"What do they say?" asked Yaakov.

"I don't know. They're kind of sloppy. Here, you try to read them." Yosef handed the camera back to Yaakov, who took it from him and stared into it once again. Straining his eyes, he managed to read the poorly spelled note to Yosef: "Sat. nite, 10:00, El-Greeba, w. da goods."

The two boys gasped. Yaakov quickly snapped a picture of Bobby the Brute's note. Then, without a word, they climbed down from the rock, made their way down the rocky hill, and ran back down the beach to their parents.

"Abba and Imma!" yelled Yaakov. "Bobby the Brute plans to steal the Torah right after *Shabbat*! We found his boat in a sea cave, and his plan was written on a note in it! You want to see it? I took a picture!" He held up his camera and showed his father the photograph that he had just taken.

"Great job, boys," answered Yehuda, after looking at Yaakov's picture. "What an excellent pair of explorers you are. Now it looks like we have what we need to convince the police that something's about to happen at El-Ghriba."

Yaakov didn't expect the police to see things his father's way. "Abba, the police don't trust our warnings anymore. First we came to them with a silly story about chasing a pirate, and then we tried to show them a boat that wasn't there. Why don't we just go to El-Ghriba and warn the people there that Bobby the Brute's coming in about two days? I'll even go there with you tomorrow morning for *Shacharit*."

Yehuda closed his mouth and appeared to think over Yaakov's suggestion for about half a minute. Then, he smiled and answered. "You know, you're right. If the people at the synagogue think they're about to be robbed, they can call the police right away, and be believed. It's a nice plan, Yaakov. Get up early tomorrow and we'll go there together."

"We'll all go," said Leah, in a determined voice. "Meanwhile, I want to *see* that *sea cave* myself. Lead the way, boys."

We're closing in on you, Bobby, thought Yaakov, as he and Yosef led their family down the beach together, toward the rocky hill overlooking the pirate's secret cave.

9 YAAKOV'S PLAN

Standing at the front doorway of the El-Ghriba synagogue, Yaakov marveled at the beauty and the artistry that he saw inside. This synagogue was designed unlike any that he had ever seen in California. Most of its walls were painted a shade of blue that reminded him of the ocean, especially as it appeared in his mother's paintings. Its ceiling was supported by thick, blue columns.

The building's main room was a spacious hall filled with rows of benches. In its center stood a raised platform, reached by two steps, where the Torah scroll was often opened and read publicly. This central platform was surrounded by rows of benches from three sides. Directly in front of it was the Holy Ark, the vault housing the oldest Torah scroll in the world. A wide, ornate balcony overlooked this main room.

Yaakov wondered how any thief could possibly manage to break into the Ark and to steal the ancient artifact that it protected. Police patrolled the neighborhood around El-Ghriba, and the building itself was heavily locked and alarmed. Yet, somehow, Bobby the Brute had hatched a secret plan to move the Torah scroll outside and to deliver it to some unknown customer. Yaakov was determined to foil his wicked plot. All that he needed was a plan of his own!

On this Friday morning, the synagogue was mostly empty. Some two dozen worshippers of various ages sat on some of the benches, with much space separating them from each other. With his father and Yosef at his sides, Yaakov recited *Shacharit*, the Morning Prayer, from an old prayer book, Yehuda wearing his traditional prayer garments, his *tallit* and *tefillin*. Though he didn't recognize all of the unfamiliar accents that he heard around him, Yaakov was able to follow most of the prayer service. Near the end, he quietly added his own personal prayer for success in stopping Bobby the Brute's plot.

After the service, most of the congregants left the synagogue, nearly all of them on their way to open the shops that they owned. Some of the older ones stayed and studied Torah texts, works of ancient Jewish wisdom such as the Talmud and Jewish law. Yosef ran upstairs and joined Rachel in exploring the balcony. Leah, Yehuda and Yaakov approached a middle-aged, kindly looking, well-dressed gentleman with a short, grayish-black beard, who sat on a bench near the Ark in the front of the room. The man seemed to be absorbed in a holy book that he held on his lap. Yaakov guessed that he was El-Ghriba's rabbi.

"Excuse me, sir," said Yehuda. "Do you speak English?"

"Yes," answered the man, in a gentle, inviting tone,

looking up from his book and extending his right hand. "Rabbi Reuven Sassoon. And who might you be?"

"Yehuda Peretz," answered Yehuda, shaking the rabbi's hand. "This is my wife, Leah, and our son, Yaakov. He's our oldest. His younger brother and sister are around here. . .somewhere." His voice trailed off as he turned and took a quick look around the room.

"It's nice to meet all of you," said Rabbi Sassoon. "What brings you here today?"

"We're on vacation from California," answered Yehuda, "but we're also on the lookout for a pirate." Rabbi Sassoon raised his eyebrows at the mention of the word "pirate."

Yehuda Peretz continued: "We have reason to suspect that on Djerba right now, there's a pirate who's traveled here all the way from the States to steal this synagogue's ancient Torah scroll."

"What?" asked Rabbi Sassoon, in obvious disbelief.

"Yaakov, show him your picture," instructed Leah.

Yaakov held up his camera for Rabbi Sassoon to see, showing him his photograph of Bobby the Brute's note. "Rabbi," said Yaakov, "yesterday my brother and I found the pirate's boat at the beach. This note was on it. We think it's his plan to deliver your old Torah scroll to someone who would be ready to pay a lot of money for it. It's the oldest in the world, so it must be valuable."

Just then, Yaakov heard a loud "bump" from behind. He turned around and saw one of his sister's rubber balls bouncing off of the synagogue's wood-paneled floor. It was a small, yellowish toy about the size of a handball. He lifted the ball and looked upward, toward the balcony. Meanwhile, his parents conversed with Rabbi Sassoon about their trip to Djerba and their pursuit of Bobby the Brute.

"Oops!" called Rachel from the balcony. "Can I have it back, Yaakov?"

Yaakov quickly tossed the ball back up to the balcony, over its railing and into Rachel's hands. He tried to do fling it quickly and without being noticed. Unfortunately for him, an elderly man sitting on a nearby bench in deep study and thought had looked up from his volume just in time to see Yaakov's throw.

"Hey, no ball in the *beit knesset!*" hollered the elderly man in a thick Middle Eastern accent, using the Hebrew phrase meaning "synagogue." "You want throwing a ball, you do it outside! This is not playroom!"

"Sorry," answered Yaakov, sheepishly. The man gave Yaakov an angry look and then delved back into his studies. Yaakov turned around and tried to listen again to his parents' conversation with the rabbi, who apparently had not noticed the bouncy ball or the elderly man's outburst.

"I'll tell you what," said Rabbi Sassoon to Yaakov's parents. "You be on the lookout for anything fishy, and so will I. If you actually see anything dangerous, let me know right away and I'll contact the police. The police will believe me. They've done a good job protecting this neighborhood for a long time, and they take any threats very seriously. Now, what are you doing for *Shabbat?*"

Over the past two days, Yaakov had wondered occasionally about how *Shabbat* in Djerba would feel. To spend an entire day – from Friday at sunset time to Saturday night – in a foreign country without turning on or off any electric devices, drawing pictures or riding in a car, was a bit daunting, especially when neither he nor his family knew a single person in all of Tunisia. Would he have to spend the whole day sitting in a boring hotel room, without even using a robot?

"We had no plans, really," answered Leah. "We were going to spend it at our hotel. It's a couple of miles from Hara Seghira, a little far to walk."

"Then come and stay with us!" Rabbi Sassoon broke out into a wide smile as he gave the invitation. "My family's used to taking in guests. We have plenty of room. A lot of tourists come here, especially in the summer. It's a short walk from our home to El-Ghriba, and there's plenty for the kids to do. Here's my address." He took a pen out of his pocket and wrote down his address and phone number on a small scrap of paper, which he then handed to Leah.

"Thank you, Rabbi," she said, as she took the paper. "We're looking forward to it."

Rachel's ball then came crashing down from the balcony again. This time, Yaakov saw the ball bouncing off one of the wood panel's on the floor, right in front of the Holy Ark. As the ball bounced, the wood panel seemed to move out of place, one end of it tilting downwards into an empty space before moving back to its usual position. It happened so quickly that Yaakov wondered whether he had actually seen something or had only imagined it. Yaakov wanted to crouch down and lift that floorboard. Maybe it really was loose. Were there other loose ones nearby? Why would there be an empty space right under the floor? Was it just a little storage space, or. . .

"Who's playing ball again in the *beit knesset*? I said

no ball in here and I mean it!" thundered a loud, upset voice from behind. Yaakov's turned around and saw his newfound elderly friend standing and pointing at him. "You! Out! And don't come back!"

Rabbi Sassoon stepped in to save the day. "Mr. Habib, please don't be upset. These are new visitors from America. They've come for a little vacation, and they're not here to cause any trouble."

"No!" shouted Mr. Habib. "They're making too much trouble now. Take the kids and go! Don't you come back here anymore!"

"Don't worry, my friends," Rabbi Sassoon assured Yehuda and Leah. "Everything's fine. I know Ovadiah Habib very well. He's been part of this synagogue for many years. On *Shabbat*, he's a lot more easygoing, and you'll get no trouble from him then."

As he walked back to the minivan in the warm morning sun, Yaakov felt his disappointment grow worse with every step. What a day to get kicked out of a synagogue! If only he had a few extra minutes in there, he could have lifted that loose floorboard and taken a quick look into the empty space that he thought he'd seen underneath it. He felt very close to cracking the last detail of Bobby the Brute's plot. A new possibility had entered his mind a few minutes earlier. No thief could just walk into a busy, guarded house of worship and steal its Torah scroll, but what if he could tunnel his way in from underground?

Immediately after buckling her seatbelt, Rachel began yapping about how high her yellow ball could bounce. She boasted of her ability to get the ball from the balcony's floor almost up to the ceiling. Of course, she reassured her parents, she would never knock out a light bulb.

"You know what happened one time?" she asked aloud. "My ball crashed down so hard that it moved a piece of wood from the floor! I even saw into the hole under the floor for about a second. Isn't that crazy? There must be a secret tunnel under there! That's what it looked like! Imma and Abba, can we go crawling into that tunnel one day?"

Without waiting for his parents' answer, Yaakov turned to Rachel and addressed her with quick speech. "Rachel, did you really see that floorboard move?"

"Of course I did," she answered, calmly. "Didn't you?"

"Yes!" replied Yaakov. "That's it! Abba! Imma! I've figured out exactly what Bobby the Brute wants to do!"

"Okay, Yaakov," said Leah, calmly, "what does he want to do?"

"It's obvious now," replied Yaakov, his voice shaking with the excitement of a new discovery. "He's dug a tunnel underground, a tunnel leading straight to the Holy Ark. Tomorrow night, after everyone's gone home, he wants to crawl in through his tunnel, break open the lock on the Holy Ark, steal the Torah scroll, carry it back through the tunnel, and then deliver it to a rich customer. It has to happen late at night, in a quiet neighborhood like this one, so he doesn't get caught. He also has to steal it quickly, before anyone realizes that somebody got into the building. Bobby the Brute expects the people at El-Ghriba to find out on Sunday morning that their Torah's missing. By then, it'll be too late. He'll be out of the country with lots of money."

"Not unless we stop him," said Yosef. "But how

can we? We don't even know where the other side of his tunnel is."

"That's okay," replied Yaakov, assertively. "I have a plan. Remember those trees along the path leading to the synagogue's entrance?"

"Yes," answered Leah.

"We'll hide behind one of those trees. We'll get there twenty or thirty minutes before ten o'clock. Tx-Rex-Mod can scan the ground near the building and find the pirate's tunnel."

"Again with the robots?" asked Yosef, sounding annoyed.

"Yes, Yosef," answered Yaakov, sharply, *"again* with the robots. Let me finish. We'll find the tunnel's entrance and wait for Bobby the Brute. Once he shows up, even before he crawls into his tunnel, we'll call Rabbi Sassoon. He'll call the police, while there's still plenty of time to stop Bobby the Brute." He paused for a few seconds. "Abba and Imma, what do you think?"

"I think you'd make a fine detective, Yaakov," answered Yehuda, as he started the early-twenty-first-century minivan's engine. "It's certainly worth a try. Now, let's head back to the Desert Star for a real breakfast."

It was hard for Yaakov to enjoy the day's sightseeing trips. Yaakov and his family explored a very old military fort, supposedly standing since 1745, and its lighthouse. Back in Houmt Souk, they visited a popular museum displaying old clothing, jewelry and the like. Signs and tour guides gave interesting historical information about the attractions of the day, but Yaakov learned none of it. Even as he packed a small bag for the upcoming *Shabbat* visit to Hara

Seghira, Yaakov could think of nothing but his plan.

10 THE PIRATE TRAP

The two Peretz brothers stood behind an olive tree lining the walkway to the El-Ghriba synagogue, huddling together in front of Tx-Rex-Mod and staring at the strange images being formed on the robot's screen. One corner showed the date and time: "Sat 5-Jul-2025 9:30 PM." Almost time to strike, thought Yaakov, moving his eyes from the underground scene on display and glancing quickly at the time. Bobby the Brute, you're about to walk into a trap that you've dug for yourself. We'll find your tunnel soon enough.

Yaakov's plan was simple enough. He had first come up with it on Friday morning, and then reviewed it throughout that afternoon and the entire *Shabbat* day. By now, he and Yosef had ironed out all the details. They would wait for Bobby the Brute to approach his tunnel, then quickly call Rabbi Sassoon to warn him of the coming robbery. The rabbi would contact the police, and the boys would distract the pirate with a robot, keeping Bobby the Brute busy until the police arrived.

The imagined capture of Bobby the Brute had played itself out in his mind again and again over the Shabbat day. Whether eating delicious Djerban dishes baked in communal ovens, strolling the old and well-worn streets of Hara Seghira, finding his seat in El-Ghriba for prayer, playing soccer with the Sassoon children and Yosef in a paved yard, or studying Torah with his father, Yaakov had found it hard to stop thinking about his upcoming defeat of a wicked pirate. Now, if only they could find that tunnel. . .

Tonight, as Rachel and her mother slept in the Desert Star Resort, the neighborhood around El-Ghriba was eerily silent. The only sound was the steady rumble of Tx-Rex-Mod's ground penetrating radar device. This clever invention, the "GPR," as Dilip Sitoop had called it last year when trying to sell Tx-Rex-Mod to a somewhat skeptical Yehuda, included a compact little probe and a set of controls attached to Tx-Rex-Mod's body. The probe was a four-wheeled device that looked like a typical toy truck. A miniature radar transmitter and antenna were attached to the probe, along with a thin signaling antenna for sending pictures of underground areas to Tx-Rex-Mod as the probe drove over them. Tx-Rex-Mod showed those underground radar images on its screen.

Yaakov carefully operated the GPR's remote control by hand, using it to drive the probe around the open space near the synagogue building, while he and Yosef searched the screen for any sign of Bobby the Brute's tunnel. After about ten frustrating minutes, Yaakov's heart began to sink. Maybe Rachel and he were both wrong about the tunnel entrance that they thought they had seen. Maybe it was time to head back to the resort and get some sleep. By now, hadn't he done all that he could have done to foil Bobby the Brute?

Just when Yaakov thought it was time to quit, he noticed an empty space on Tx-Rex-Mod's screen that looked like an underground passageway. Before he could say anything, Yosef spoke up.

"Abba, guess what?" called Yosef in a whisper that sounded loud, as whispers go. Yehuda Peretz was leaning against the next tree along the walkway, joined by Digital Drudge (in case, as Yaakov had carefully pointed out, anybody got thirsty during the sting operation) and AutoShoveler (because one could never know when a digging robot might come in handy).

"What is it, Yosef?" he asked, looking up and stopping himself from falling asleep.

"We found it!" He pointed to the tunnel on Tx-Rex-Mod's screen. "Bobby the Brute's tunnel!"

"Great job, boys!" said Yehuda in a low voice. "Now, why don't you try to find its entrance?"

Yaakov continued driving the GPR probe, using the images on Tx-Rex-Mod's screen as his guide. Yosef helped him to navigate the device, until the narrow tunnel on the screen suddenly widened to a large hole.

"Okay," remarked Yosef, in a hushed tone, "I think we've just found the opening. But where is it above ground? It's so dark outside that I can't even see the probe."

"No problem," replied Yaakov, quietly. He pulled his BotConv from his left pocket, attached it to his left ear, tapped it, and continued whispering. "Digital Drudge, bring me a flashlight."

Despite the darkness, Yaakov could see Yosef roll

his eyes as the robot slowly began walking from Abba's tree to the boys' tree. "Couldn't you have just asked Abba to bring it?"

"Abba's tired," snapped Yaakov.

A moment later, Digital Drudge arrived. Yaakov took a flashlight from the cardboard box full of tools, drinks and other items that Digital Drudge carried on its foldable metal tray. He turned on the flashlight and shined its wide beam of light in front of him, toward the area from which he thought he'd heard the sounds of the probe's motor. Yaakov waved the flashlight around for a few moments, searching for the small four-wheeled machine that would mark the entrance to Bobby the Brute's tunnel. Finally, he spotted the GPR probe in front of a desert shrub, a low bush similar to the ones that dotted parts of the southern California desert.

"Abba, I found it!" he whispered quickly to his father. "Bobby the Brute's using a little bush to hide his tunnel."

"Yaakov, turn off your flashlight!" Yosef hissed, before Yehuda could respond. "Someone's coming!"

Yaakov immediately switched off the light and squinted into the darkness ahead. He soon noticed a lanky, shadowy figure approaching from the distance. Quickly, he pushed a button labeled "IR Cam" on Tx-Rex-Mod's control panel, turning on the robot's infrared camera.

The infrared camera was designed to create pictures using infrared radiation (also known as "IR radiation"), invisible light waves given off, to some degree, by every person and animal in the world and by nearly every object in the universe. Hot objects generate more intense IR radiation than do cold objects, and heating an object is a way to increase the amount of IR radiation that it generates. People, animals and objects give off IR radiation constantly, both during the day and at night. Because an IR camera uses IR radiation, rather than visible light, to produce pictures, it can photograph objects on even the darkest of nights.

Yaakov pointed Tx-Rex-Mod's IR camera toward the distant stranger, and then zoomed the image on the robot's screen until it seemed close enough to show the details of his face. The man photographed had a scraggly little beard (not trimmed or shaven for several weeks), and beady eyes. The pirate was on his way!

"Abba," called Yaakov, as loudly as he could while still whispering, "we've caught Bobby the Brute on camera!"

"Let me see," answered Yehuda, leaping over to Yaakov and Yosef's tree. He looked at the face on Tx-Rex-Mod's screen. "That man looks like just like him. Send that picture to my phone, Yaakov. I'm calling Rabbi Sassoon."

Yehuda took his smartphone from his pocket and dialed Rabbi Sassoon's number. "Rabbi Sassoon? *Shavua tov,*" he greeted the rabbi with the Hebrew expression meaning "Good week." Then, he continued, "We're in front of El-Ghriba. Remember that pirate we told you about on Friday morning? We can see him approaching the synagogue right now. You need to call the police." He then listened for the rabbi's reaction, while Yaakov pushed a few buttons on Tx-Rex-Mod's control panel, transmitting a stream of IR images to his father's phone.

"Yes, I'm serious," Yehuda told the rabbi. "I'm

going to send you some pictures. Just a second." He pushed a few buttons on his phone, and then held it to his ear again. "Fine," he continued, "make it a three-way call."

Yehuda turned on his phone's speaker. Yaakov overheard Rabbi Sassoon give the local police a very quick description of the crime about to take place. An officer on the other end then told Rabbi Sassoon that the police would be on the scene right away. The rabbi thanked the officer and then hung up. He then thanked Yehuda, wished him a good week once again, and ended their conversation.

"Bobby the Brute's getting pretty close to that bush," said Yosef, pointing at the now zoomed-out picture visible on Tx-Rex-Mod's screen. "He'll be in and out of it before the police get here. Somebody has to stop him from getting into it in the first place. I say we grab him right now, tie him up and give him to the police as soon as they come. Did Digital Drudge bring those ropes like it was supposed to?"

"Yosef," said Yehuda, "don't try anything. It would be too dangerous for you to start up with a pirate."

"But not for a robot," suggested Yosef. "In fact, it would be easy. Digital Drudge seems just the right size to fit into that little tunnel. We could send it in stop Bobby the Brute, and then he'll waste a few minutes trying to get the robot out of his way. By the time he gets past Digital Drudge, the police will be here!"

Yaakov was worried by the idea of sending his very own homemade robot, which he had worked for a full year to build, into a secret tunnel to fight a dangerous criminal. What if Bobby the Brute managed to demolish Digital Drudge? All of Yaakov's hours of hard work in the garage, and of careful study of electronics and robotics manuals, would go to waste. On the morning of his tenth birthday, Yaakov had sat down at his desk and begun planning how to construct his very own personal robotic servant. He had spent his eleventh year dreaming of owning a machine that could make his life easier by following simple voice commands. To put Digital Drudge together, Yaakov had mastered the use of both basic building tools and sophisticated electronic components (although, sometimes, the robot's light emitting diodes flickered on and off unpredictably). He would never forget his eleventh birthday party, when he had demonstrated the robot for the first time by ordering Digital Drudge to cut a piece of cake and bring it to him. His family and friends had watched in awe as Yaakov's home-built robot delivered the snack. How could he now send his very own robotic butler, made with his own hands, into a hole in the ground to be wrecked by a ruthless thug?

"Yosef," answered Yaakov, "if Digital Drudge gets in Bobby the Brute's way, he'll do more than try to get past my robot. He'll destroy it! Remember what almost happened to AutoRiser when it got in Pete Weasel's way?"

"Who cares?" asked Yosef. "Catching Bobby the Brute is more important."

Though the thought made him nervous, Yaakov realized that Yosef was right. After all, what was the point of chasing Bobby the Brute halfway around the world if they were just going to let him get away? How could he live with himself if a whole Jewish community lost the oldest Torah scroll in the world, just because Yaakov refused to give up his robot?

"Digital Drudge, walk straight ahead." Using Tx-Rex-Mod's IR images as his guide, Yaakov gave his robot several additional commands that guided it toward Bobby the Brute's tunnel. Eventually, Digital Drudge reached the bush that concealed the formerly secret tunnel's entrance. "Now climb into that hole in the ground."

Digital Drudge crawled into the hole and disappeared. Yaakov, Yosef and their father waited.

After about five minutes, a black car approached the synagogue and parked about fifty feet away from it. Its headlights immediately turned off, and the car just sat in place. Nobody opened any of its doors. That's strange, thought Yaakov. Late at night, a black vehicle drives up to a synagogue that's about to be robbed, and the driver simply shuts off his headlights and sits there. Quickly, quietly, Yaakov pointed Tx-Rex-Mod's IR camera at the strange vehicle and took a photograph. The picture clearly showed the vehicle's Tunisian license plate, and a driver whose head was covered by a ski mask. Who would wear a ski mask in a Middle Eastern country on a hot summer night? wondered Yaakov. He – or she – must have something to hide.

At 9:48, by Tx-Rex-Mod's clock, the IR camera showed Bobby the Brute finally reaching the hole that he had dug in the ground. He got down on his hands and knees, pushed aside some of the nearby desert shrub's branches and then started crawling inside. Soon, Bobby the Brute's frustrated shouts could be heard coming from the direction of the hole.

"Hey, what is this thing? Get this heavy piece of junk out my way! Come on!"

"Service with a smile, sir!" came Digital Drudge's

loud, metallic voice. "Would you prefer the orange juice or some raspberry tea?"

"What is this, a robot? Get out of my tunnel!" screamed Bobby the Brute. The pirate's shouts were now accompanied by the sounds of his pounding on Digital Drudge's metal body. "I'll throw this thing out of here myself! I'll tear it limb from limb!" Yaakov wanted to do the same to Bobby the Brute. His anger rose further with the sound of each blow. He began to tremble, and felt as if he were about to cry.

Yaakov soon felt his father's hand on his shoulder. "Yaakov," said Yehuda, " I know you're upset. You should be. But you're a very wise and resourceful young man. You can build yourself a new robot in no time. I know you can."

"But it won't be the same," answered Yaakov, barely able to hold back his tears.

Yehuda looked down at his son and smiled. "No, it won't be the same. It'll be a lot better."

Just then, the sounds of approaching sirens were heard in the distance. Though he continued to pound on Digital Drudge without a stop, Bobby the Brute's shouts began to take on a desperate tone. With police sirens growing louder by the second, the mystery car's engine and headlights suddenly turned on. The car made a quick U-turn and drove off into the night.

"Abba," said Yosef, "Bobby the Brute might still get away. What if he gives up on his plan, climbs out and runs away?"

"He won't get away with that," answered Yaakov, with a steely determination. "He's trapped." Yaakov dashed to the tree that his father had used a few minutes earlier as a hiding spot, and looked straight at

AutoShoveler. "AutoShoveler, follow those loud screams. Go over to the hole where those screams are coming from, and start digging a new hole right next to it. Fill up the first hole with the dirt from the second hole."

"And hurry up!" shouted Yosef, giving the robot a good, hard kick in its back.

As the three Peretzes watched on Tx-Rex-Mod's IR screen, AutoShoveler sped toward Bobby the Brute's hole and began filling it with dirt.

"Hey, who's shoveling that dirt in my face?" came Bobby the Brute's next holler. "Stop that!"

Bobby the Brute tried to climb out of the hole while AutoShoveler repeatedly threw shovelfuls of dirt into the pirate's face. The pirate found himself stuck between a badly damaged Digital Drudge that blocked his way into El-Ghriba and a steady stream of dirt that rained down on him from AutoShoveler's shovels.

While Bobby the Brute struggled, three police cars parked in front of the synagogue, sirens flashing. Yehuda and his sons greeted the six arriving officers and pointed them to Bobby the Brute. Two of the officers approached the pirate's tunnel and pulled him out of it, while Yehuda began telling the others all that he knew about the pirate's crime.

Bobby the Brute refused to quiet himself, even while being led to a police vehicle. When the pirate was close enough to be seen clearly, Yaakov thought that he saw him tap a little black box a few times, before a burly officer grabbed it from him. What was that thing? A video game system? A calculator?

"Wait until Rahulla finds out!" yelled Bobby the Brute, as the same officer shoved him into the police car's back seat. "Then you'll all be in trouble!"

11 HOME AT LAST

The "FASTEN SEAT BELT" sign came on with a loud ring, jolting Yaakov out of his nap. "Rahulla Allijabulla!" he blurted, opening his eyes and straining for a moment to remember where he was. After a disoriented second or two, he remembered having buckled himself into the aisle seat that morning, before sunrise, for takeoff from the Djerba airport.

Yaakov and his family had spent the past twelve hours on Aharon Sapir's private jet, which now began its descent toward Santa Barbara. Looking past his parents, Yaakov could see the Mojave Desert through the airplane's window. For a few moments, he squinted at the light brown desert sand that seemed to stretch forever, trying to spot the hole from which he had so recently pulled a buried treasure.

"Rahulla *what?*" asked Leah, from the cushioned seat next to Yaakov. "What are you talking about, dear?"

"Imma," answered Yaakov, "I just had a really

weird dream. There was a huge, puffy birthday cake in front of me, even taller than Abba. It was an ice cream cake, and it almost looked too good to eat. You, Abba, Rachel, Yosef, and a whole crowd of other people were standing around me, shouting 'Cut the first slice! Cut the first slice!' over and over again. I climbed onto a little stool with a knife in my hand, reached up to the top of the cake, and started cutting into it. All of a sudden, guess who surprised everyone by popping out of it? Rahulla Allijabulla! And he wasn't even invited!"

Yehuda, seated on Leah's right, turned to her and began to explain. "Rahulla Allijabulla," he told her, "is the name of the strange man who drove that black mystery car on the night after our first *Shabbat* in Djerba. The Tunisian police identified him by his car's license plate. When they questioned Bobby the Brute, he told them that he'd been hired by Allijabulla to steal El-Ghriba's ancient Torah scroll that night, and to deliver it to him right then and there. Allijabulla was willing to pay $50 million for it."

"Wow," said Leah, "you could buy three or four houses in L.A. for that kind of money. *Medium-sized* ones, too!"

"Not only that," continued Yehuda, "but Bobby the Brute told the police that they'd never find Rahulla Allijabulla. Never."

"But they found him, didn't they?" asked Leah, as the plane tilted downward, its descent toward the Santa Barbara airport growing a bit steeper. "I mean, when you and the boys came back to the hotel that night, you told me that the police were out looking for the owner of some strange, black car. Now that I think of it, you did tell me his name. It was so long and exotic that I couldn't remember it until now. Didn't they end up finding him?"

Yehuda simply shook his head. "When we left Djerba this morning, Allijabulla was still on the loose. On that first night, the police actually did manage to find the black car. It was an old, gas-powered Lincoln Town Car, built about twenty years ago. They found it just on the other side of the bridge connecting Djerba to the rest of Tunisia and the African continent."

"I remember when you told me that part," replied Leah. "But you got a few calls from the police since then, didn't you? You never told me about those calls."

"Well, there's not much to tell. The police tried searching Allijabulla's address – at least, the one printed on his driver's license – and just found an old, abandoned tenement building. It wasn't exactly the mansion you'd expect to house a guy who could offer $50 million for an ancient relic. That's the last I heard of him. Whoever drove that car did a good job of running away and hiding. He could be anywhere by now."

The conversation soon died down, and the Peretzes prepared themselves for landing. Yaakov deftly placed a stick of gum in his mouth and began chewing hard, to help his ears withstand the change in air pressure that always came with landing. He loved to fly, but hated the earaches that it gave him.

Half an hour later, Yaakov found himself standing on the shiny, black asphalt of a runway in Santa Barbara. The pleasantly warm summer morning, typical for southern California, was a welcome relief after two weeks in the scorching North African desert. The children helped their parents carry their bags to Mr.

Sapir's waiting limousine. Aharon Sapir stepped out of the vehicle and instructed two waiting porters to load the Peretzes' bags into the trunk. He then greeted the Peretz family warmly, congratulating them on their successful defense of the Djerban Jewish community's ancient treasure.

"Don't worry about your lost robot," he reassured Yaakov, placing a hand on his shoulder. "The truth is that those things come and go, like anything else. You have an exciting future ahead of you. I know it."

Back at home, the children dashed in through the front door of their house, dropped their bags right away and raced outside to the backyard. Yaakov certainly had missed the wide grassy space behind their house, and could tell that Yosef and Rachel had missed it, too. It felt good to stretch his legs, finally. Yaakov slid the glass door a little bit further open, following his younger and smaller siblings. He ran so quickly that he almost crashed into the unexpected figure standing in the center of the yard: Buzzing Bill.

"Uh-oh," said Yaakov, nervously. "I left it on the whole time! I hope its battery isn't dead by now."

"Why don't you try it?" offered Rachel. "Tell it to do something."

Yaakov played with the robot's controls for a few minutes, checked its signal records, and realized that this robot had monitored radio signals from the Djerba area for the past two weeks, without a stop. He then remembered the night that Bobby the Brute had been caught. The pirate had fumbled with a little black box before the police snatched it from him. It was quite possible that Bobby the Brute had sent someone an urgent, last-chance signal. Maybe Bobby the Brute had sent a secret message, and maybe that message was now stored in Buzzing Bill!

Yaakov remembered that he was not allowed to use Buzzing Bill to listen to other people's private signals, not even those sent by criminals. But maybe Bobby wasn't such a brute, after all. Could he have managed to send a message through some sort of public channel?

"Imma!" called Yaakov, hurrying back into the house. "Can I spend some time today going through Buzzing Bill's records? I think it picked up something important. Bobby the Brute might have sent somebody a message before they took him away! I just have to check on. . ."

"Forget it," she interrupted, holding up her right hand and giving Yaakov a stern look. "You need a break from robots for a while. And you're done chasing pirates. They caught Bobby the Brute, and that's that. Now, go to your room and pack up your backpack. You're late for camp."

If you enjoyed Yaakov the Pirate Hunter, *kindly share your thoughts with others by writing a review on* Amazon.com. *Thank you!*

Also, be sure to read the other books in the Peretz Family Adventures series!

Book 2: Yaakov and the Treasures of Timna Valley

Book 3: Yaakov and the Secret of Acra Fortress

ABOUT THE AUTHOR

Nathaniel Wyckoff was born and raised in the beautiful San Fernando Valley of southern California. From an early age, he was profoundly interested in reading, writing, telling, and listening to stories.

His storytelling career took flight with the births of his children. They now enjoy all kinds of tales, many of which are told to them by their father. Nathaniel's first novel, *Yaakov the Pirate Hunter*, was inspired by his son's request for a story about robots.

In addition to writing, the author also enjoys studying his Jewish traditions, reading, playing the accordion and the piano for his family, playing games and sports with his children, and taking his family on hiking trips, camping trips and other adventures.

Join my Readers Club, for giveaways and updates on new books:
http://www.peretzadventures.com